BALKAN BEAUTY, BALKAN BLOOD

Writings from an Unbound Europe

■ □ ■ □ ■

BALKAN BEAUTY, BALKAN BLOOD

MODERN ALBANIAN SHORT STORIES

Edited by Robert Elsie
Translated from the Albanian

NORTHWESTERN UNIVERSITY PRESS

EVANSTON, ILLINOIS

Northwestern University Press
www.nupress.northwestern.edu

The authors or their representatives hold the rights to the original stories, which were
first published in Albanian in the following sources: "Stars Don't Dress Up Like That,"
in *Yjet nuk vishen kështu* (Elbasan: Sekjo, 2000); "The Men's Counsel Room" ("Oda e
burrave"), in *Lulehëna* (Peja: Dukagjini, 1997); "The Loser," in *I humburi* (Tirana:
Dituria, 1992); "The Slogans in Stone" ("Parullat me gurë") and "Adonis," in *Tregime*
(Tirana: Onufri, 1997); "The Couple" ("Çifti"), in *Parrullat me gurë* (Tirana: Albimazh,
2003); "The Snail's March Toward the Light of the Sun" ("Marshi i kërmillit drejt dritës së
diellit"), in *Marshi i kërmillit* (Peja: Dukagjini, 1994); "The Secret of My Youth"
("E fshehta e rinisë sime"), in *Nëntori* 2 (Tirana, 1990); "The Pain of a Distant Winter"
("Dhembja e një dimrit të largët") and "Another Winter" ("Një dimër tjetër"), in
Një dimër tjetër (Tirana: Naim Frashëri, 1986); and "The Appassionata" ("Apasionata"),
in *Vepra letrare* 6 (Tirana: Naim Frashëri, 1972).

"The Secret of My Youth" and "The Pain of a Distant Winter" were previously
published in English in *Description of a Struggle: The Picador Book of Contemporary East
European Prose*, Michael March, ed. (London: Picador, 1994).

Printed in the United States of America

10 9 8 7 6 5 4 3 2 1

ISBN 0-8101-2336-3 (cloth)
ISBN 0-8101-2337-1 (paper)

Library of Congress Cataloging-in-Publication Data

Balkan beauty, Balkan blood : modern Albanian short stories / edited by Robert Elsie.
    v. cm. — (Writings from an unbound Europe)
    Contents: From Stars don't dress up like that / Elvira Dones — The men's counsel
room / Kim Mehmeti — From The loser / Fatos Kongoli — The slogans in stone /
Ylljet Aliçka — Adonis / Ylljet Aliçka — The couple / Ylljet Aliçka — Ferit the cow /
Fatos Lubonja — An American dream / Stefan Çapaliku — The mute maiden /
Lindita Arapi — The snail's march toward the light of the sun / Eqrem Basha — The
secret of my youth / Mimoza Ahmeti — The pain of a distant winter / Teodor Laço —
Another winter / Teodor Laço — The appassionata / Dritëro Agolli.
    ISBN 0-8101-2337-1 (pbk. : alk. paper) — ISBN 0-8101-2336-3 (cloth : alk. paper)
    1. Short stories, Albanian—Translations into English. I. Elsie, Robert, 1950– .
II. Series.
PG9665.E54B38 2006
891.99130108—dc22

                                                                    2005036777

CONTENTS

■ □ ■ □ ■

EDITOR'S INTRODUCTION

The first book in Albanian was written in the year 1555, yet creative prose in that language is very much a twentieth-century phenomenon. Albania was ruled for five centuries by the Ottoman Empire, which banned Albanian-language schooling, Albanian-language writing, and Albanian-language publishing. It was only in 1912, when the little Balkan nation finally received independence, that Albanian began to be used in all walks of life, including publishing and creative writing, on more than just a sporadic basis.

The earliest serious collections of Albanian prose date from the 1930s with the works of Ernest Koliqi (1903–75), Mitrush Kuteli (1907–67), and Migjeni (1911–38). Indeed the years 1933 to 1944 mark a golden age for writing in Albanian, fleeting as it was. This promising decade was brought to a swift demise at the end of the Second World War, when Communist partisans took power and set up a primitive Stalinist regime in Albania, which lasted unbridled and unimpeded to 1990. The existing intellectual community was terrorized into submission from the very start. Most writers either fled abroad, were executed, or were sentenced to long terms in prisons and concentration camps. Albanian literature, indeed Albanian culture, had been silenced.

Despite the atmosphere of fear and intimidation which reigned in Albania for almost half a century, the new system made great strides in providing basic education and services for the population and in creating stimuli for a new generation of proletarian writers. Nonetheless, the vast body of writing which was churned out in the fifties and early sixties proved to be sterile and highly conformist in every sense. The subject matter of the period was repetitious, and simplistic texts were constantly spoon-fed to readers without much attention to basic elements of style. It is no wonder that many works of socialist realism remained in the bookstores gathering dust. Political education and fueling the patriotic sentiments of the masses were considered more important than aesthetic values. Even the formal criteria of criticism, such as variety and richness in lexicon and textual structure, were demoted to give priority to patriotism and the politburo's message. The approach taken was designed to reinforce revolutionary fervor and to consolidate the socialist convictions of the new man. Whether it attained its objective to any extent is doubtful. It was insufficient, at any rate, to stimulate talent and to ensure literary quality, and thus, in the long run, it did not succeed in satisfying the aesthetic needs of the Albanian reader.

The second generation of postwar Albanian writers increasingly came to realize that political convictions, though important within the context of the Albanian society of the period, were not the only criteria of literary merit and that Albanian literature was in need of renewal. The road to renewal was facilitated by a certain degree of political stability and self-confidence within the Albanian Party of Labor despite worsening relations between Enver Hoxha and the Soviet leader Nikita Khrushchev.

One turning point in the evolution of Albanian prose and verse, after a quarter of a century of standstill, came in the stormy year of 1961, which, on the one hand, marked the definitive political break with the Soviet Union and thus with Soviet literary models and, on the other hand, witnessed the publication of a number of trendsetting volumes, in particular of poetry: *Shekulli im* (*My Century*) by Ismail Kadare, *Hapat e mija në asfalt* (*My Steps on the Pavement*) by Dritëro Agolli, and in the following year *Shtigje poetike* (*Poetic Paths*) by Fatos Arapi. It is ironic to note that although Albania had severed its ties with the Soviet Union ostensibly to save socialism, leading Albanian writers, educated in the Eastern bloc, took advantage of the rupture to try to part not only with Soviet prototypes but also with socialist realism itself. The attempt made to broaden the literary horizon in search of something new inevitably led to a literary and of course political controversy at a meeting of the Albanian Union of Writers and Artists on July 11, 1961. The debate, conducted not only by writers but also by leading party and government figures, was published in the literary journal *Drita* (*The Light*) and received wide public attention in the wake of the Fourth Party Congress of that year. It pitted writers of the older generation such as Andrea Varfi (1914–92), Luan Qafëzezi (1922–95), and Mark Gurakuqi (1922–77), who voiced their support for fixed standards and the solid traditions of Albanian literature and who opposed new elements such as free verse as un-Albanian, against a new generation led by Ismail Kadare (b. 1936), Dritëro Agolli (b. 1931), and Fatos Arapi (b. 1930), who were cautiously in favor of a literary renewal and a broadening of the stylistic and thematic horizon. This march along the road to renewal was finally given the green light by Enver Hoxha himself, who saw that the situation was untenable and declared that the young, innovative writers seemed to brandish the better arguments. Though it constituted no radical change and certainly no liberalization or political thaw in the Soviet sense, 1961 set the stage for a few years of serenity and, in the longer perspective, for a quarter of a century of trial and error, which led to greater sophistication in Albanian literature. Topics and techniques were diversified, and somewhat more attention was paid to formal literary criteria and to the question of individuality. By the late 1960s and early 1970s, literary prose had thus recovered to an extent and was making good progress, though firmly within the framework of the official doctrine of socialist realism. Many of the most successful prose writers of the late twentieth century have their origins in those years of cautious experimentation: Dritëro Agolli, Teodor Laço, and Ismail Kadare.

Ismail Kadare is the only Albanian author to have been widely translated and to enjoy an international reputation. His talents both in poetry and in prose lost none of their innovative power over the last four decades of the twentieth century. Kadare's courage in attacking literary mediocrity within the Communist system, and later—though subtly—in attacking the political system itself, brought a breath of fresh air to Albanian culture. His works were extremely influential throughout the seventies and eighties, and for many readers, he was the only ray of hope in the chilly, dismal prison that was Communist Albania. Much to the regret of the editor, Mr. Kadare chose at the last moment not to authorize publication of the three tales of his which had originally been foreseen for inclusion in this anthology with those of the other authors.

When the "Socialist People's Republic of Albania" finally imploded in 1990, what remained was chaos—a sub-Saharan economy and little direction or leadership on the part of writers and intellectuals. Half a century of isolation from the rest of Europe had taken its toll.

Though a reasonably broad range of Western prose had been published in Kosova, only leftist writers and classic authors of centuries past had been available in Albania itself. Contemporary prose from other European countries or the Americas was unknown. There was now much to catch up on, and readers understandably turned away from their own writers to prefer new, albeit often shabby Albanian translations of the contemporary foreign literature of which they had been deprived for so long. The early 1990s were years of disorientation for Albanian writers because they had no tradition upon which they could build. Initially they imitated the styles and themes of Italian, English, American, and French prose, and it is only in recent years that a fresh and unfettered Albanian literature has emerged and crystallized.

It is as yet difficult to generalize about the characteristics and concerns of contemporary Albanian prose, but much of it naturally reflects the Albanian experience, bitter as it has been over the last few decades and up to the present. After a brief and mostly unsuccessful attempt to come to terms with the horrors of the past, writers are turning increasingly to reflections on the very diverse aspects of contemporary life in Albania and Kosova, and in particular on themes of Albanian emigration.

Albanian literature—especially modern Albanian prose—remains little known in the outside world. This is due primarily to the glaring lack of literary translators from Albanian into English and other foreign languages but also to the traditional isolation from which Albania and its people have suffered. Two hundred years ago, historian Edward Gibbon described Albania as "a land within sight of Italy and less known than the interior of America." At the cultural and literary levels at least, little has changed.

The present collection of Albanian short stories is but an introduction and is not intended to mirror the full range of Albanian prose. It nonetheless endeavors to reflect the best of modern writing from the last three decades, in particular the 1990s. Included are prominent and well-established authors from Albania and from the large Albanian communities of Kosova and Macedonia as well as some relative newcomers to the literary scene. After decades of muteness, Albanian writers have many tales to tell. It remains for me to thank all the authors included here for their kind cooperation. Particular thanks also go to Janice Mathie-Heck, of Calgary, Canada, for her vital assistance with the preparation of the manuscript.

■ □ ■ □ ■

BALKAN BEAUTY, BALKAN BLOOD

■ □ ■ □ ■

FROM STARS DON'T DRESS UP LIKE THAT

Elvira Dones

IF I WERE NOT SO DEPRESSED, I MIGHT EVEN BE HAPPY. IS IT RAINING out? I can't really see what is happening. I might be happy if this insidious pain were not driving me crazy. But in the final analysis, it is probably better the way it is. I am going back to where I swore I would never return. There is nothing to keep me in this country anymore, so I am off. I wouldn't have left if they had just let me live my life. No, it's not the rain I hear. It's the roar of the sea that swells and softens bones.

It will break my heart to hear you scream when you see me. Oh Mommy, what I would give to be able to throw my arms around you! But I will have to endure your screams without being able to comfort you, to stroke your head lying on my breast. Shhh, Mommy, I'm home now. It's all over, the pain is gone. I am back and there is no more need for sighs or regrets about things you once promised me. We can put up with anything if we only stay together: with venomous thoughts, the treacherous sun, and even the icy blue color of the moon. I will not be able to say a word, and God knows how I will be able to endure it.

I was determined not to go back, certainly not as down and out as I was at that time, or as disfigured as I am now. I didn't want to go back at all. I wanted to stay here, although there was nothing keeping me in this country. You are so stubborn, you'll never get anywhere in life. Right, I am stubborn, or rather, I was. Leila, you'll never stand on your own two feet unless you're untarnished.

In the daytime, my determination was crystal clear and definitive. But nighttime made a traitor of me. During the very few nights that I actually slept like other people do, I dreamed of returning Back Home.

I would get off the ferry; it was the kind of sunny day you only get Back Home. Enough sun to drive you mad. I would disembark, breaking into tears, and throw my arms around my mother, her tiny figure standing in front of me with her head resting under my chin.

"Leila."

"Shhh, Mommy. See, I'm back."

"Oh Leila."

Around us as we embrace are stray dogs roaming through the garbage strewn in decay all over the jetty. Children with beautiful eyes are prancing about. Suitcases fly through the air in the direction of waiting relatives, and policemen with faded uniforms and envious glances are scratching their butts. There is enough dust to powder your eyebrows and the sky is deafened by the merciless honking of horns.

We stand there with our arms around each other. My mother's eyes are staring into my soul, and my eyes are looking out at the scorching heat. In my dreams I often arrive Back Home in summer and when I awake, I'm really happy. I glance around my little room, the venue of my nightmare, and am enthralled by the homecoming and the reunion. It is still night. I go back to bed and try to sleep and return to the solace of my dreams. I know that I will change my mind in the morning and will revert to my decision never to go back. But it is still night, and I long to savor the illusion.

I close my eyes and the story begins where I left it. My mother, myself, my grandmother who hobbles on her right leg, Aurora who is still alive and has not stopped growing, my father following closely behind us with all the luggage, all of us under the inquisitive glance of the lazy and noisy city. We have thrown our arms around one another, and with my left hand I can feel Aurora's beating heart.

"Leila, I've got so much to tell you," she says to me passionately.

She takes hold of my hand, still measuring the beat of her heart, and stares into my eyes. I look straight ahead out of fear that my glance will betray me.

"You will tell me how it was, won't you? About all the things you learned and about all the good-looking men you met over there."

"Of course I will, Aurora, as soon as we have time."

"Tomorrow?"

I laugh and try my best to sound cheerful. It is a strange feeling because I actually am happy. After all, this is a happy dream.

Grandmother mutters something or other. She has only one front tooth left and her tongue wraps around it like a piece of pastry. We don't understand anything she says, and the three of us laugh— Aurora, Mother, and I. Grandmother imitates our laughter, a bit uncertain at first, and then bursts into a giggle of her own. This saves me from the embarrassment of it all. We set off for our elusive home. Behind us we can hear Father gasping, cursing the heat, and juggling the bags from one arm to the other. We set off for nowhere. Then my dream comes to an end. Once and for all.

There are no passengers in this part of the harbor, in front of the ferry. A man, around fifty-five years old, is staring at his shoes and smoking a cigarette, which has turned to ashes right to the filter. The ash is bent downward and from one angle it looks like an extension of his finger. The man's hand is shaking, as is his head with its tufts of gray hair at the side. His glance remains fixed on the tips of his shoes. If he were to look up, he would be betrayed by the tears dripping onto the asphalt without ever touching his cheeks. But the man does not want to weep. There will be enough time for that when his wife screams in horror and despair. The man already knows he won't have the strength to endure it. For the moment, he is just trying to keep control of himself. Finally, the ash falls from the cigarette, part of it blowing away as dust and the rest landing on the tip of his right shoe. The man rolls the filter through his fingers until he grasps it by the end. He has no matches and stuffs the butt in his pocket. A policeman taps him on the shoulder.

"You can go aboard now. This way. Come along with me."

The policeman is young, about ten years older than Leila. He gives the other two officers a sign and they come forward to get the coffin.

"No," replies the man, giving a cough, and stares at the three officers, one after the other, as they stand erect with their arms dangling at their sides. "I'll get it myself."

"Are you sure?" the first one mutters, but his voice remains unheard. The man picks up the coffin and lugs it toward the gangplank. They follow. They give him the keys to a cabin, but he shakes his head and continues down toward the bow of the ship.

FROM STARS DON'T DRESS UP LIKE THAT

"You'll be better off here, Daughter. We can go in later if you want."

The three officers follow, keeping right behind him. They can't get a word out. The man places the coffin carefully on the deck, whispers something to it in his language, and then turns to them. The officer in charge returns his passport, his driver's license, the police documents, the autopsy, the authorization from the hospital, the authorization from the police in Back Home, the photos of Leila before she turned into a corpse, and photos of Leila as a corpse.

"This is where our job comes to an end."

His lips are quivering and he endeavors to enunciate more assertively. The other two look out to sea toward the seagulls and ships, and at the rust and oil shimmering on the surface of the water.

"You understand me, don't you?"

"Yes, I do."

"Do you have . . . other children?"

"I once did." The three men exchange glances. One of them shrugs.

"I had another daughter. I buried her two years ago."

"Oh God," the youngest officer murmurs to himself, "what a day!" He would like to get away but is ashamed and, instead, stuffs his hands in his pockets and tries to look as if he does not understand what is being said. "God, what a day!"

"Sir, we would like to express our deepest sympathy. You know, if you ever come back this way . . or if there is anything we can do for you . . . I have two sons, twins of kindergarten age . . . I mean, I'm a father, too. . . ."

The officer in charge is overcome with emotion, and the other two are now trembling more than the tufts of gray hair on the man with the coffin. They shake hands with him, one after the other. He looks at them, a withered, shriveled old man whose voice seems to have left his body completely and taken refuge among the plywood boards of the coffin. He is not able to thank the officers. "Why do you abandon me now, stupid voice?" The muscles in his neck grow tense as if he wants to say something, but nothing comes out. He gives up and wants only to be left alone. If the scene lasts any longer, he knows he will scream and Leila beside him will be frightened. He doesn't want to frighten her.

The officers go their way. The man sits down on the deck, searching through his pockets for his tobacco and cigarette paper. It's time for a smoke and he begins to roll himself a cigarette. "This will get me back into shape."

Silence from inside the coffin. Two seamen shout something about an approaching fishing boat.

It takes him a long time to roll the cigarette, which he eventually lights.

"We'll be leaving soon, Leila."

The stevedores are arguing about how to load the cars onto the ferry. The man smokes and seems to have found salvation in the strong tobacco. What luxury, to have a whole ferry to yourself. You don't even see that in the movies. He and Leila are returning home, and there is no one else on deck.

When he went to book their passage for the return journey, the men at the ticket office had looked askance at him.

"You are the only passenger returning to Back Home. Do you know what is going on in your country? There's war—everything is in flames. Are you sure you really want to go back? Hundreds and hundreds of desperate people are arriving here every day and no one is traveling in the other direction. No one wants to set foot in that country. You understand me?"

"There was war when I left the country, gentlemen, and there will be war when I get back. I know what I am getting into."

They looked at him as if he were crazy. He had to explain to them that the coffin was not empty and that his daughter's body could wait no longer. She had left home three years ago and he had now come to take her body home. After all, he had to get her under the earth before the body began to putrefy and stink. The officer was shaken and made a gesture as if to say, "Enough." He said he wanted to inspect the documents. It was a complicated business with a corpse. . . . On the wall behind the officer was a large color poster of a young woman surrounded by three children, posing like a brood hen with her chicks.

"We're leaving now and we'll have a rest when we get home. After all, what's keeping us here, Leila? What do you think?"

I know that he can see everything. He's hiding here somewhere around the jetty. The police searched for him everywhere but they will never find him. He is here somewhere, I can feel it. I have a good nose for him now. I always know where he is and what he is thinking.

FROM STARS DON'T DRESS UP LIKE THAT

Too late. I have learned to protect myself from him but only now that I no longer need to do so. Our love was a morbid affair, somber as the unlit mineshaft into which I had slid without a candle or a spade. I had gotten involved not knowing that there was no way out. The mineshaft was so dark that I lost not only my way but also my very being. Now, staring at my coffin, he is abject, torn from within and put to shame by the killer instinct he detected within him. He is mourning me here, mourning me, and yet he's even afraid of the smoke of my father's cigarette. What a coward!

I must have patience. The only thing I have left to do is accompany my body home, where I will take one last look at my mother and one first look at Aurora's grave. Then I will vanish from the face of the earth. It is Monday, a day which has always brought me luck. Monday, March 5, 1997. I can see my body cut into slices like a watermelon and I can see the man who did the job. He groans and takes care not to come out from behind the mast where he is hiding. Imagine what it is like seeing yourself in a coffin, knowing you will never again touch a human being, never again drink a cup of coffee or comb your hair. How strange it is to see the man who ripped through your body with a knife and not to rise before him like a ghost and—as in the Greek tragedies—to howl and vanish in the night.

He will suffer from his deed, but not to the extent that he would ever give himself up to the police. He knows that the investigation will soon be closed. For a while, they will continue to search for the murderer of a prostitute, and then the case will be filed away. There is no point in public expenditures for a whore from Back Home, they will think. And what a rotten bunch these people from Back Home are anyway. They come here, live on welfare, and we have to support them. Couldn't we have had better neighbors than these people from such a godforsaken country? But you can't choose your neighbors any more than you can choose your relatives. If there is bad blood among them, there is nothing you can do about it. They are there for life. If you have a bad neighbor, you can do only one of two things: either you get your hands on him or you move out. But countries cannot move out. They can move and change other things: laws, strategies, armies, presidents, allies, and even their names if they want, but they can't move away. And to get control of that pack of thieves, well, you can't really.

The file will gather dust in the corner of some office. In it are pictures of me working the streets in those awful clothes I hated. And there are other pictures in the file of my body, slaughtered like a lamb.

The man from the criminal investigation department took the pictures while humming a song that was on the charts at the time. He bent over me, taking a close-up of my neck, with his feet pressed against my thighs, and all the time, he was humming the tune. The phone rang in his pocket.

"Ciao. . . . No, I can't right now. Why, is it urgent? We'll talk tonight. I'm busy now. Someone's murdered a whore, and is she in bad shape! The guy really made mincemeat out of her." Did I actually look like mincemeat? I am not a prostitute and never really was. Thank God I always kept my papers with me in a pocket. The police found them so they were able to identify me and contact my parents.

"OK, no problem. We'll talk tonight. All right, we'll go for dinner. Something simple, all right? I haven't got too much cash at the moment. What about a pizza? Fine, ciao. I miss you, too. Bye."

"Oh," sighed the photographer. "*Che strazio 'sta donna.*" He turned off his phone and continued taking pictures until someone gave him the OK to stop.

Father wipes the sweat off his forehead. He moans as the gangplank scrapes and rumbles. I'm so sorry, Father. I know you weren't expecting such a blow. Thank God that corpses don't blush. How could I ever have looked you in the eye? I never wanted to go home alive. How would I have been able to lie to you all? How would I have endured your tenderness?

"Leila, my love, my treasure. Leila, my treasure, you're all my joy, the best child in the whole world."

"My teaser," he used to call me, and I repeated the expression as a child when I had learned to pronounce whole words. My parents laughed. My mother, who always smelled of soap, threw her arms around me. Later, when I grew up, it was, "Leila, my treasure, take care of yourself." I'll do my best, Dad. And now . . . I had become the teaser of all those men after me, lying on me, and I tried to convince myself over and over that I was their treasure.

"Who knows how much you've suffered, my daughter. Whatever did they do to you, my love? Say something. How can I take you back to your mother this way, Leila, my child?"

FROM STARS DON'T DRESS UP LIKE THAT

The ferry departs, rocking to and fro like an old man trying to get out of bed. It coughs twice and sets off. The sea is calm. Father bends over and kisses the plywood boards of the coffin.

"Will you invite me Over There, Leila, once you get married to Fatos and have a beautiful house of your own, like in the movies?"

"Of course I will, Sister. I promised you, didn't I?"

"And I'll grow up and be as good as you are."

"You're good already, Aurora."

"You're the best sister I could ever want, the most beautiful sister in the world."

When I first set out across the sea, Aurora came with me, arriving in the same harbor from which Father and I had set out a few hours ago. There were light showers that day. It was the last moment I would ever see my sister, but I didn't know it at the time.

Six months later, they sent me pictures of her corpse. Her eyes were still wide open.

It was the day after I saw the pictures of Aurora's body that I consented to work as a whore. And to perish, bit by bit, from that day on.

I hope you never smile again. I hope you will never even remember your name, murderer! I pray that your memory be deleted, be washed away by the waves of the sea. How else could your soul endure the horror when you recall what you have done? "I love you so much," you once said, "I would die for you." But you are still alive and I cannot even spit in your face.

We drift away upon the gentle sea, Father and I and this godforsaken ferry. No road is more gentle than the sea.

THE MEN'S COUNSEL ROOM

Kim Mehmeti

HAD I WANTED TO PLAY THE ROLE OF A PRETENTIOUS WRITER, I WOULD have begun this tale by describing the hairpin road leading up to the village. To do so, I would have to insert one of those boring flashbacks which writers use when they go into detail about various incidents which took place in various localities long ago. Many writers assume that they can awaken interest that way, though in fact they are only deluding themselves and others. Their various narrative descriptions only show that they are concentrating on the past because, compared to the present, it can be embellished with so many lies that it becomes convincing, even for the authors themselves.

No, no. You cannot force me to go into some superfluous descriptions of Syla's Grove, which lay parallel to the hairpin road that led from the mill at the foot of the hill up to the school building at the entrance to the village. Were I to describe the oak trees and bushes growing at the two sides of the road, which was so narrow that the heavily laden mules would brush against the brambles, I would inevitably have to reveal the secrets of our youth. Those, in turn, had to do with the initial fuzz and hair between our legs which showed that we were gradually turning into men. Hiding behind the thick bushes, we proved our manhood by frenetically milking the source of the white drops which fell onto the fresh grass. Nor would I want to write anything about Bala's widow and her little bedroom window through which we climbed, one by one, to give natural proof of our manhood, that is, up until the night when all the villagers were saying their prayers during the holy month of Ramadan. It would be an even more despicable revelation were I to tell you the story of Galin, who, just after he had entered the bedroom of Bala's widow for the first time, came out as pale as wax and moaned to us that, as soon as he was lying naked beside her, his body went into a spasm, the muscles in his legs went stiff and, already limp and moist, he did not even manage to caress her smooth thighs, not to mention anything else. He wiped the sticky drops of sperm off his belly, and it was only later, when he had revived, that he was able to tell us about the insults hurled at him by the young widow, who was trying to get her fill of our hot bodies, inexperienced though they were in such matters. Then it was my turn, and I took the brunt, when Bala's widow, hot and flushed in unsatisfied lust, turned to me bitterly before I had even finished undressing and cried, Hey, snot face, you better get your act together better than that last guy, or I'm going to whip your butt with a clump of nettles." And then . . . well, I would not even dare to go into all the details about how I got into bed with her, groped for her swollen breasts, how my hand glided down her bare belly, and . . . touched her thighs, oh. . . . My hands had only begun to stroke her hot thighs when a couple of warm sticky drops fell onto my belly. My manhood had collapsed, like the defensive walls of a fortification. Something sweet and somehow inexplicable deceived my body into giving way and coming, without even having felt the warm insides of her body. She gave me an infuriated look, as if she were going to slap me. "Don't worry, a real man doesn't abandon the battlefield that easily. I'll show you what love is!" I proclaimed, covering her in kisses. Lying on her, I was determined to carry on to the point of collapse. I don't know how long the indescribable ecstasy lasted or why I didn't hear the whistling of my companions outside her window who were trying to let me know either that it was someone else's turn or that one of the villagers was about to discover the reason why Bala's widow kept her bedroom window open and the lights turned off during the early hours of twilight. What I do remember, though there is no need or reason to go into all the details, is sad and rather embarrassing. When I jumped out of the window onto the road outside, I found myself face to face with the brother of the late Bala, who had died after two years of marriage, leaving his widow to seek solace in the pleasure of our young bodies. My mother gave me such a beating and covered me with such insults that I still don't know how I managed to survive her rage.

KIM MEHMETI

By the next day, to make things even worse, news of the incident had spread through the whole village. The consequences were terrible. My family got into a dreadful clash with the Mulajs. I managed to ignore all the curses and insults which I received from my father, my uncle, and all my other relatives, with the exception of the women of the family, who gave me embarrassing glances and could obviously not imagine how I could possibly even go out into the courtyard after such a scandal. I was more worried about the conflict between the two families. It is an embarrassing story that casts light on the concerns of that age and on Bala's fair widow, whom we had sent packing, after having gone through that first phase of manhood, i.e., jacking off in Syla's Grove. Two weeks later, the brother-in-law returned the widow to the bosom of her family, and we slunk off to Syla's Grove once more. The elders of the village had mediated and put an end to the animosities between our family and the Mulajs.

There would be no point in my writing about the bitterness of my companions. For several days they would not talk to me at all and made me responsible for what had happened, even though they had been just as deeply involved in the matter as I had. They accused me of being eternally voracious and of sacrificing regular daily meals for an ephemeral moment of gluttony. I did not even try to convince them that you could not take an instant of ecstasy with you. There is absolutely no need now for me to go into the details of how shocked the villagers were that some shameless individuals like us had stooped to such depths while they were saying their prayers. Once Bala's widow was sent packing, we were faced with a long period of male deprivation.

Had I the tendency of certain pedantic writers who concentrate on long, detailed descriptions and other nonsense which I consider superfluous, I would have to mention Dalip's cornelian cherry tree, which was situated to the left of the road, just before the penultimate bend on your way up to the village. A description of it and of the surrounding area would lead me inevitably to refer to matters which are better not put to paper, or rather, should they be put to paper, then only in indirect terms. But I dislike allusions and prefer to avoid revealing the truth by means of incomprehensible symbols. At any rate, no one really knew why they called it Dalip's cornelian cherry. It was a term that gave rise to various and sundry interpretations and speculation, among which is the story of a certain Dalip. He was an old man who had stopped there hundreds of years ago to take a pee on a tree trunk and had died in excruciating pain from a bite he suffered, having opened his trousers right over a viper's nest. They also tell the story of another Dalip, who, according to the villagers, was a handsome young man. No one really remembers all the details, but they say he hanged himself from a branch of the cornelian cherry tree after his first night of marriage, apparently because his bride had a bleeding nose and a spider emerged from between her legs at the very moment he was making love to her. It is a story you can believe or not. If you don't believe it, well then, you're free to make up another one about Dalip's cornelian cherry tree. Like every cornelian cherry on earth, it is the first tree to blossom in spring, a harbinger of the songs to be sung by maidens upon their covered balconies and of swallows up in the sky. The blossoms were a sign that life was shortly to return to Syla's Grove.

Dalip's tree was also the spot where the men of the village deposited the placentas when their wives had given birth. The custom had been going on for centuries and probably stemmed from the fact that there was no brook anywhere near the village. No one took the time to hike down into the valley and hurl the placenta into the waves of the river in order to ensure that the new mother would produce enough milk and that the child would prosper. They simply wrapped up the paunchy round piece of meat dripping in blood, which had surrounded the embryo until it turned into a human being, and placed it carefully at the foot of Dalip's cornelian cherry, only to return home concerned, but also overjoyed at the birth of their child. The rite was always accomplished in the early moments of twilight. The next morning, the father returned to Dalip's tree to see if the viper there had in fact eaten the placenta which had been placed under it the night before. He was the only person in the village who ever actually saw the serpent, which he insisted had the eyes of a baby, a body several meters long, and two or three hairs on its head. They also said that at midnight it began to hiss in a deafening manner. This was a rare occurrence. Everyone believed that a child born on a night in which the viper hissed would never be able to shut his eyes from sunset to sunrise and would suffer terrible agony and die if the viper did not swallow three eggs, each of which had to have two yolks. This terrifying being, of which all the inhabitants of the village were somehow proud, would leave uneaten only the placentas of those women who had given birth to stillborn or short-lived children or to children stemming from the semen of another man, that is, of women who had been unfaithful to their husbands. It was a terrible blow for a father to find the placenta untouched the next morning at the base of the cornelian cherry tree. He would not know whether his wife had given birth to a child that would not live long or, even worse, to a child of the blood of another man who had brought shame upon his house and permanent damage to his manhood. Many children are born in our village, and fortunately there have been few cases in which the viper living at Dalip's tree refused to eat the fresh meat because it sensed that a wife had deceived her husband. More often, the child died at an early age, as the snake had portended to the parents by not eating the placenta.

It would be tasteless of me to mention the case of Balan, who one night, full of pride and joy, took the placenta out in the early hours of the evening after the birth of a son. The lad was so indescribably handsome, healthy as an apple, that even today, when the women of the village refer to him, they spit two or three times in the direction of their feet and say, "Allah be with him!" Very few of the villagers were willing to talk about Balan, and even fewer were willing to call to mind the sorrowful moment the next day when he went out to Dalip's cornelian cherry tree and froze with horror. On the ground before him was the uneaten placenta, still dripping in blood. He stood there pale and somber for a moment but then had the presence of mind to pick up the placenta and hurl it as far away as he could so that the other villagers would not find it. But did it really matter that the other villagers did not know what he knew? He returned home with poison in his heart, though he managed to conceal his emotions from his young wife. He hoped that it would be a case of a short-lived offspring rather than, God forbid, the result of his wife's infidelity. But was it easy to live with the fact that the heir whom he had longed for would depart from this world after such a short stay? Of course not. Yet it was certainly not easier for him to live with the thought that the blood of another man was flowing through the veins of that little being who would call him daddy and that he was wasting his love on the fruit of foreign semen that had dishonored him and the property that belonged to him alone and to no one else. Only poor Balan knew what it meant to live with such a fate, and as such, if nothing else, it would be an elementary lack of taste for me to carry on about the feelings of another man as other writers, who are only trying to make fun of their readers, often do.

I shall therefore not even endeavor to describe how Balan spent night after sleepless night staring at the baby in the hope of finding some similarity to him, some sign that his blood was flowing in the child. Nor do I propose to describe the whole gamut of emotions which the poor man suffered, although I must admit openly that I find such reticence difficult because I am thereby robbing my fantasy of a chance to graze on lusher pastures and perhaps indeed give definitive proof that God does not do what people think or imagine.

To make a long story short, Balan's son grew and thrived. He survived measles and whooping cough, and it was now time for him to be circumcised. "This child will be the death of me," Balan had said to himself from time to time ever since he saw his son, or rather the child he called his son, take his first steps near the well. The child grew and Balan worried. But the belly of his wife grew, too. She was pregnant with a second child. Within Balan grew a mixture of anger, joy, and sorrow. On the night that the second child was to be born, Balan sat at his wife's bedside, wiping the sweat from her brow. When her agony had become such that she was riveted to her bed and when she had the feeling that every bone in her body had been broken, he leaned toward her and whispered in her ear, "If you do not tell me who the father of the child sleeping in the other room is, I will force you to eat all the placenta, which is going to come out of you at any moment." The wife forgot her pain, stretched her arms out to him and stammered in a weak voice, "They tricked me! Oh Balan, that he grew of foreign seed in my womb does not mean that I would not have preferred yours, but I had no other choice. They told me it was the only way for me to save you that night when they summoned you to the Men's Counsel Room. It was that bastard Asim who told me that I would never see you alive again if I did not agree to give myself to him. The government had accused you of serious crimes and only the village elders could save you." Balan groaned in pain and agony. It was as if the baby were pushing its way out of his body and not out of his wife's.

It would be senseless to bother you with Balan's story any longer. After all, I don't want to give an argument to those writers who assert that a storyteller must garnish and embellish a tale which could be told simply in order to create the impression that it is terribly complicated to write about the deeds of mortal beings. In short, it would go much too far to bring forth all the details describing the state in which Balan found himself on the night of the birth of his second son. He felt no pride or joy. His brain was flooded with thoughts that kept him mute and silent. It was the memory of that certain evening which robbed him of all his joy. It was so vivid in his imagination, as if it had been last night and not years ago when his wife lay on her side to feed the baby which had just emerged from her womb. Yes, the elders had summoned him to appear that evening at the Men's Counsel Room. It was certainly no small matter to be summoned at his young age to the place where good and evil were judged, where proceedings were held and sentences passed. Some were deprived of their honor as men, and others got it back after it had been tarnished by someone else. Every word spoken in that room was measured carefully because it echoed throughout the village. Some men would then be admired and others would be despised. He did not know what had given him the honor, after several years of marriage. But he was rightly proud. In that night he would be witness to some important decision which the village elders, the wisest of their community, would take. His companions would later envy him and would listen attentively whenever he spoke. They would no longer measure him with the same rod as they had that spineless Balan who had no brothers and who had an old fool for a father whom everyone, small and large, made fun of. He was not the Balan who had grown up on his mother's warm lap and who had been fed crumbs from almsgivers, which she had received and stuck in her pocket for him to make sure that her only son did not grow hungry. He was now being invited to the Men's Counsel Room to hear counsel from persons whose word was not to be contradicted. How often he and his friends had looked from a distance at the pale light shining in the big windows of the Men's Counsel Room. How often he had seen villagers standing, quivering, on the main square of the village to wait for a decision pronounced by the cleverest and most illuminated brains of the community. Balan set off before darkness had covered the village, happy but at the same time apprehensive that he might make a mistake and interrupt someone at the wrong moment. He entered the room and shook the hands of the sage old men with their gray beards. He greeted them all according to custom. They told him that they had invited him to listen in on their counsel and to learn from their keen sense of judgment because the day would come when the old men would lose their physical and intellectual capacities and would have to be replaced by younger ones. "And they consider you worthy to replace them," Balan stammered to himself in joy. For all the pleasure and talking to himself, Balan missed out completely on what the stern old men had said as they cast their eyes down at the colorful patterns on the carpet. He returned home late, around midnight. He lay beside his wife, who was quivering strangely, but he heeded neither her quivering nor the tears on her cheeks. He felt a need to tell her all about the honor he had been given by the village elders. He talked and talked until he finally realized that his wife's tearful eyes were closed. And now, this night, too, when his wife admitted to him that her firstborn child had been fathered by Asim, who had appeared one night in her room and lied to her, saying that Balan was in great peril and that only she could save him. She had submitted to him, had put her arms around him as she would around her brother, around one of the most respected men of the village whom no one would ever think of mistrusting. Now, years later, Balan recalled that Asim Dalini had not been present that night long ago at the Men's Counsel Room and had subsequently never again received an invitation to take part in the consultations. It was only now that Balan realized that all of those gray-bearded old men had participated and assisted in the treachery because they knew he was defenseless as the only male in the house. The men who were wont to stroll through town with worry beads in their hands and their noses turned up, always ready to pronounce judgment on the sins of others, had made a mockery of his esteem as a man, the only cherished possession that Balan had.

So you see, there are things which are better not told in public and, as such, I am not entirely sure whether I should reveal to you what happened that night when Balan's wife gave birth to her second child. Balan wiped the sweat off her brow. When she fell asleep, he went into the other room, where his wife's first son was slumbering like an angel. It was only in the early hours of the morning that he managed to fall asleep. He spent the whole next day with the mother

and her newborn baby. The next evening, he set off for Dalip's cornelian cherry tree and returned home late at night, long after midnight.
His wife had not noticed his long absence because she was anemic
and exhausted and, in her anguish and trepidation, had fallen into a
profound slumber. She noticed his presence when he kissed her af-
fectionately with a, "Sleep tight. You have two sons who are worthy
of your love." They both woke at the same time the next morning.
"Are you going to go out and see if the viper at Dalip's cornelian
cherry has eaten the placenta?" asked his wife. "No, I was there last
night until it crawled out of its nest. I saw with my own eyes how it
ate the fresh meat from your womb," he replied. The conversation
was then interrupted by shouting which became louder and louder.
The villagers were running down to the end of the village. Balan
rushed out after them to see what had happened. There, slumped
against the trunk at Dalip's cornelian cherry tree was the lifeless body
of Asim. His face was smeared in blood. From his swollen mouth
hung a piece of paunchy meat. It looked as if he had hastily tried to
swallow it and had choked to death. The villagers wrapped the body
in a white sheet and took it back to his home, from which one could
hear the moaning of the women and the whining of the children.
That evening, a lamp was lit in the Men's Counsel Room. All night
long, the elders discussed the event, which had shaken the whole
village. Balan looked once again toward the light shining in the Men's
Counsel Room and went to take a pee.

I mentioned earlier that I am not the kind of writer who is able to
embellish a tale properly and, in fact, I am not even interested in all
the details which might make it more intelligible to the reader. This
is perhaps a reflection of my inability to express in words everything
which is swirling around in my brain. For that reason I will not even
endeavor to describe the village *hodja* who, while carrying out his daily
routine, complained to the villagers that he had found a talisman with
suras from the Koran that had been thrown at the mosque. He had
made it for the infertile women so that they would once again be able
to bear children. When he bent down to pick up the little piece of
folded paper written in holy Arabic script, he got dizzy and collapsed
at the entrance to the mosque. When he woke up, he found himself
beside a female corpse which soon thereafter turned into a mole that
gave a squeak and burrowed its way into the ground.

It would be quite superfluous for me to recount all the commotion caused in the village by the news that the *hodja* had lost his voice and was no longer able to say his five daily prayers. Instead I will tell you exactly what was said by old Salushe, who is in fact the main reason why I recalled my old village and its inhabitants, burdened as they are by the monotony of their daily pursuits. To put it briefly, old Salushe, who is still alive and who dwells in the first house to the left when you come back from the village fountain, at the junction with the path leading up to the Men's Counsel Room, was wont, whenever she saw light in the room used by the village elders, to cup her crotch, massage the flaccid flesh between her legs, and stutter, "Your wisdom and the places I'm rubbing in my hands have one thing in common. The older they get, the more spunk they lose, and they don't even notice the world around them!"

FROM THE LOSER

Fatos Kongoli

THERE COMES A DAY IN YOUR LIFE WHEN YOU HAVE THE IMPRESSION that you have paid your dues to the world, the cycle is complete, and there is no more reason to ruminate upon the past, in particular when your life has nothing of value to offer. "What then?" one might ask.

Nothing. Just a confession.

One morning a couple of months ago, a friend of mine, Dorian Kamberi, a mechanical engineer and father of two children, boarded a freighter called the *Partisan* and sailed across the sea with his family. If I had not had second thoughts at the last moment, I, too, might be living in some refugee camp in that dreamland called Italy, or somewhere else in Europe, together with a horde of my compatriots. But at the last minute, as we were sitting on deck squashed like sardines, I told Dori that I was getting off. It is possible that he did not even hear what I said. After the trials and tribulations of our journey from town to the ship, a veritable Odyssey, my words must have sounded absurd. If anyone other than my friend had been beside me, he would have hurled me into the sea. Dori said nothing and just gave me a blank stare. All the while I could feel the warm pee of his little son, whom I was still carrying on my shoulders, trickling down the back of my neck.

My hesitation must have been obvious to everyone. I am sure that, at that moment, my voice and my face expressed exactly the opposite of what I was saying. Even a small attempt on Dori's part to dissuade me would have sufficed for me to abandon the decision I had just taken, not really even knowing why. It was not a question of homesickness. I felt nothing at all, and my mind was as void as the expression on Dori's face. He made no move to stop me, and I disembarked, my neck still moist from the pee of his little son. I sat down on an edge of the wharf and looked back at the final groups of refugees scrambling to get on board. When the ship set sail and had reached the point where the faces on deck could no longer be seen, I felt a lump in my throat. With my head between my hands, I began to sob and then had a long crying spell. I did not realize at that moment that it had been years since I had last cried. My soul was parched and I had long thought that nothing more on earth could move me to tears. Someone passing by put his hand on my shoulder and said not to worry, there would be another freighter coming in the afternoon. . . .

I returned to my neighborhood at nightfall. No one had seen me leave and no one saw me come back. Dorian Kamberi's departure with his family became known the next day. It was not the subject of much talk. Some criticized him, some praised him, and others were jealous. I paid attention to the gossip much like a thief who has taken part in a robbery and listens to the news of its discovery. For the first time in the forty years of my existence as a bachelor, I had a secret to keep within me. It was possibly the only secret that my town had not found out about. And it never would have found out, had I not decided to make this confession. No one would really have been surprised to learn that I had departed and boarded a freighter to disappear from the face of the earth. But that I should make the tedious journey, get on the ship, and then disembark all of a sudden, no, no one would have believed that. Even Dori, if he had indeed heard what I said, would never have thought it possible that I would really get off. Perhaps he thought that, with my usual sluggishness, I would have been more of a burden to him than his family, and therefore made no attempt to stop me.

Nonetheless, there I was. The next day, my feet carried me out to the cemetery. You might have thought that it was the grave of some loved one or some sort of nostalgic contemplation which had impeded my departure. Alas, this is not true, yet I have great respect for graves and for nostalgia. Indeed, I am envious of those for whom such notions are important and provide stability, like the force of gravity, as a basis for action. For myself, I feel I am somewhere beyond gravity, cast off and abandoned in a black hole of disdain. Nostalgia was an ephemeral luxury for me. Such were not the motives behind my aborted departure or behind my visit the following day, for the first time in my life, to the cemetery. For everyone and from every point of view, I was and am a loser.

Gray clouds hovered over the town the next morning. My thoughts were with the refugees at sea. My parents—I live with my mother and father in a two-room apartment plus kitchen—did not even bother to inquire where I had been the day before. They were used to such absences and had long stopped asking me where I was going and what I was doing. My return home at night was sufficient for them to get a good night's sleep. Thus, my thoughts were with the refugees. I was worried about them because of the bad weather, yet there are certain biological processes within the human body that take place independent of one's emotions. I was starving. I got dressed and after a brief and muffled "Morning!" from the doorway, leaving my parents to their coffee in the kitchen, went out.

I do not think there is any place on earth quite as dusty as our little town. There is dust everywhere: on the flat cement roofs of apartment buildings, on the tiled roofs of private houses, on the sidewalks, and on the flowers poking up in the only park in the center of town. It is everywhere, like icing sugar sprinkled on a layer cake in the baker's showcase window. It powders your hair the moment you go outdoors, deposits itself in your ears and nostrils, gets into your lungs and follows you everywhere, to the café, the restaurant, and even into bed. I was about ten years old when they constructed the cement factory on the riverbank on the outskirts amongst the hovels of the gypsy population. It was a construction from centuries past, said those in the know, and produced more dust than it ever did cement. The old people said that it was at that moment that the town's slow death began.

"You could already be across the ocean," I thought to myself with a shudder as I strolled down the sidewalk. The whole place looked incredibly dingy on that gray March morning, so dingy that I almost broke into tears. "You fool!" I said to myself. "What have you done?" I went straight to the café. Normally I would first have gone to the Riverside Snack Bar to still my hunger, but there had been rumors circulating recently that its owner, Arsen Mjalti, a onetime foreman at the cement factory, had been using meat of dubious origin for his grilled sausages. There was a lot of gossip about it, ranging from rotten meat taken from dead cows to dog meat, and the gossip was confirmed by numerous cases of diarrhea among his customers who, unable to come up with proof to give Arsen Mjalti a good thrashing, simply boycotted the establishment. As a result, the snack bar was now only patronized by a few good friends of his and by the occasional traveler passing through. It is possible, however, that the rumors had been spread by a few envious individuals, for it was said that the onetime foreman was making a fortune and that, if he continued, he would have enough money to buy the famed Hotel Dajti in Tirana.

The café was empty. To my good fortune, behind the espresso machine on the counter there was a row of bottles of Scanderbeg cognac, which I had not indulged in for quite some time. The waitress at the bar knew exactly what I wanted before I could even open my mouth. She handed me a double cognac to start with and then made me a coffee. I went over to the window with a glass in one hand and the cup of coffee in the other. Here, customers drank standing up at little elevated tables. Without further delay, I downed the glass of cognac in one swift gulp. I felt terrible and was on the verge of tears, hardly able to stifle what would have been a ridiculous scene in front of the waitress. It was only the third double cognac that saved me. Calmer now, and confident that the beast clawing at the depths of my being had been vanquished, I ordered a fourth cognac, which I began to sip slowly, together with the coffee that I had not yet touched. There were few people out on the streets. Either the heavy clouds of the morning sky had discouraged them from going out, or, as it was a Sunday, they were still sleeping or lying in bed staring at the ceiling, certain that there was nothing of interest to venture outdoors for. Everyone seemed to be sleeping the sleep of the dead. I wanted to go down to the town square and scream at them: "Wake up, my fellow citizens. Everyone else is gone and you have been left behind!"

I stayed put, sipping away at my cognac until the glass was empty. I ordered a fifth one. I now felt that smooth, velvet sensation under my skin. If you have never tried it, you cannot understand what it is like. The world is back in keel and your mind grows sharper. A clarity about right and wrong wins the day in your soul, or rather a feeling of righteousness, and you are in a position to make clear decisions without complexes and without trepidation. It was at that moment that I decided to take a walk out to the cemetery. I had never been there before, but at that moment, it seemed like the most natural thing, something I just had to do and indeed should have done long ago. I was shocked at the thought that I had never been. I did not know, as I was finishing my fifth glass, that it was there that I would meet a person from town known as Xhoda the Lunatic. If I had, I would not have gone.

He was emerging from the graveyard by the gate built into the hole-pocked red brick wall, which was almost as high as a man. For this reason, I did not see him in time. Otherwise I would have avoided him. Suddenly there he was in front of me, much like a vampire looming in a nightmare. He was unshaven, his hair unkempt in the wind. Xhoda was wearing a military cloak, which was open at the front, revealing his hairy chest. For a moment, I froze under his piercing eyes. He was holding a long iron bar in his hand. He stood there before me, looking as if he were in deep thought, and gave me an angry glance. As I looked into his bloodshot eyes, I remembered the old saying that even a madman gives way to a drunk. But I was obviously not drunk enough or he not mad enough. At any rate, I could only get into the graveyard by passing him.

I recovered from my initial shock, but I was afraid that he was going to lash out at me. If he had done so, I could only have ducked and raised my arms to protect myself, just as I had done on several occasions in the past when he, then the school principal, had been on the lookout for a victim among the pupils, upon whom to vent his rage. I had been among his preferred targets. This time he did not strike me, either with his hand or with the iron bar. He did not call me a bastard or a scoundrel. He just glared at me with his bloodshot eyes and I, unable to resist his glance, took flight.

Xhoda the Lunatic was the first person ever to call me "incorrigible." I will always remember the scene in his office when he hurled this accusation at my father who, for his part, as a sign of agreement, gave me a slap in the face to convince me that I really was the person the principal accused me of being. If the principal had gone further, alleging for example that I was a born criminal, although I had only just turned fourteen at the time, my father would have agreed and slapped me in the face again. My father was not really a bad fellow, but at that moment I hated him more than I did anyone else, even the principal.

I do not remember the circumstances under which Xhoda first struck me with his cane. It was probably for one of the usual reasons at small-town schools for which caning is tacitly accepted and for which the teachers know full well that the parents will not make a fuss. The beatings took various forms, but all of them involved care being taken not to leave any marks on the pupils' bodies. I did not get beaten until the fifth grade for the simple reason that my teacher for the first four grades did not believe in corporal punishment for her children. In the fifth grade we got new teachers whose habits were quite different and, after being passed around from one to the other, we came to realize that we had been really lucky during our first four years of school. Then it began. I had never been beaten at home because, as I wanted to say, my father was a placid fellow. The real head of the family was my mother, but she was not in the habit of beating children either. My classmates, most of whom were the children of simple working families, got beaten all the time, both at home and at school.

I now have a lump in my throat when I think back at the horror with which I faced the moment I was to be caned. I had no doubt at all that the time would come. What I did not realize was that my first punishment would be doled out by the principal himself. He was a terrifying man, the only one whom even the rowdiest boys would run away from. When he stood before the school, the teachers could sense the unease and fear among the mass of pupils, and I often had the impression that they were more frightened of him than we children were. I imagined their fear as being more or less like mine, that is, a fear of the cane in the principal's office, where I had never been and where I hoped never to be taken. I was well aware of the fate awaiting any boy to be sent there.

My first caning was traumatic. I do not remember the reason for it, so it had no particular punitive effect. It could have been a complaint from one of the teachers about my being too loud, or a protest from one of the girls whose braids I might have pulled. There might have been other reasons, too . . . anything. I might, for instance, have grinned at the wrong moment or moved from my place in line when the principal was holding a speech before the school. But it may also simply have been my turn because I was one of the rare boys in town who had not yet felt the principal's cane on his back.

After being yanked by the ears and the hair around my temples and having been slapped several times, an experience I would often undergo, I left the principal's office without a tear. Dazed, I rushed home to tell my father. I was at the age when children believe that their father is the strongest man on the planet, the person who will protect them and solve all their problems. This was the origin of my trauma. I had not really known my father up to that time and had imagined him different than he was. It would take a few more years for me to come to realize that his wimpy, servile reactions, which struck me to the core, were not simply a result of his sluggish nature.

The following day, he accompanied me to the principal's office. Had I suspected that he was going to degrade himself to that extent, I would never have told him about the beating. I would have preferred being beaten ten times a day rather than see the terror in my father's eyes. Such humiliating scenes would repeat themselves often, with the only difference that, later, my father, who had never struck me, would become accustomed to doing so and would exercise this activity with passion every time he was summoned to school by Xhoda the Lunatic to learn of my mischievous deeds. This went on until I reached the seventh grade, when Xhoda pronounced the fatal word "incorrigible" and I really got caned. From that time on, I think I became incorrigible for good.

But let me return to that day when, after the first beating, I made the fatal discovery: my father was not strong at all. My father was a coward just like the rest of them, like the teachers and everyone else who quivered in Xhoda's shadow. I was twelve years old at the time, and still in the fifth grade. Now, almost thirty years later, I can state with conviction that I wept more tears that afternoon than I did for the rest of my life. And I ran away from home. They found me in Tirana the next day asleep on a bench in the park across from the Hotel Dajti. I was in a state of exhaustion, starving and frightened. I did not know that this naive disappointment was to be but the first of a whole series of disappointments. Yet I experienced none of them with such tragic intensity as this one because, for me, my father was now dead, and the damage done could not be repaired. Xhoda had destroyed the vision I had cherished of my father, and so I decided, in my manner, to take revenge.

We were living at the time in the same apartment—two rooms and a kitchen— where we live now. I had and have one sister who is five years older than I am, but she plays no role in my story, if I can call the mediocrity of my earthly existence a story. The chronicle of my life is, to be certain, mediocre. It is the story of a man who never was and never turned out to be anything, an anonymous existence melted into the anonymity of an obscure neighborhood in an obscure town, even though it is not far from the capital city. My sister spent most of her time away from home. When I was little, she was at a boarding school of the teacher training college and, later, when she got a job, she was appointed as a teacher in a village in the north of the country, where she remained.

My apartment building is situated near the center of town. Across the road, on the other side of the park and the paved square, there is another apartment building, on the ground floor of which are various food stores, a fabric shop, a tailor, and a café. The café has made the apartment building and the whole square well known in town. It is here that the most spectacular brawls between individuals and rival groups have taken place. The town did not take them particularly seriously, probably because the inhabitants considered such brawls to be a normal part of everyday life, just as it later became normal to sit around and watch films on television. There was no television in town at that time, and yet there was no lack of news. Most of the inhabitants were of the impression that dust played a decisive role in all newsworthy events. In conjunction with the vapors of alcohol, it drove my fellow citizens to folly. They are a passionate bunch and are excessively jealous—two things which do not fit well in an atmosphere of peace and quiet. In addition to this, most of them are workers with strong arms and ready fists. What else could be needed to make headlines? The news in town was, however, never put to writing. Interested sociologists are advised to contact the local authorities, who, I hope, might still have records of such events. Perhaps they even have a file on a certain Thesar Lumi. That is me.

I say "perhaps" because it seems to me that I am making a bit too much of myself, thinking that there might be a whole file on me.

I was and remain thoroughly insignificant and, in deeming possible the existence of such a file, I certainly do not dare compare myself to those who are worthy of such an honor. I, however, take pride in believing those who insist that one does not have to be important to have a file. All one has to do is cast a shadow on this earth. I would be more than happy if this were the case, for it would mean that, at a time when I considered myself nonexistent in this world, there were others who were of a different opinion. And I am grateful to them.

To give myself a pat on the back, I will thus assume that there was a file on me. I do not know what could possibly have been written in it and most likely I will never find out, but one thing I can say for sure: the real facts, which might in one way or another be construed as criminal activities, are missing. They cannot be in the file because, when I committed them, I was still a child. I committed them at the time when, for no comprehensible reason, my father suddenly submitted to the will of Xhoda the Lunatic and I lost all my respect for him. Thus, I decided to take revenge.

At this point in my narrative, I should mention Vilma, or rather my memory of her. Vilma no longer exists. She has been gone for a long time.

My brain tends to confuse time periods so that I am not sure whether Vilma was already every boy's dream when I was a child. I do not know whether she had already been destined at that age to play the role of an apple of discord in a town of rowdies. My sluggish mind has difficulty piercing the layers of past years, that curtain of fog behind which the universe of my childhood and my vision of Vilma lie. I was but a child when I got to know her, although I thought myself a man. Boys grow up quickly in a little town like that.

I can see her beyond that curtain of fog. There she is, standing behind the wrought-iron fence. She always used to stand there, watching passersby out on the street. Today, behind that same black fence, passersby can now see Xhoda the Lunatic sitting on a bench with the wild eyes of a madman. He stations himself there like a guard dog. His madness consists of the fact that he believes his daughter is still behind the fence and, with an iron bar in his hand, he is poised to attack any potential foes. Poor fellow. He did not realize that Vilma was untouchable. He did not know that his petrifying shadow would not have been able to defend her against anyone. There was something else that protected Vilma, and woe to him who dared to touch but a strand of her hair. Even if he had deployed a hundred guard dogs around the house or had sent a hundred hounds out to follow her in the streets, they would not have protected his daughter as well as Fagu.

It is exasperating. It drives me mad. I want to talk about Vilma, yet it is the specter of Fagu that rises before me. I want to recall her shining eyes, the color of the deep blue sea, but before me I see those black eyes, always full of anger. With difficulty I manage to forge my way through the thick fog in search of that placid, intelligent face, and I only come across Fagu's eternally gloomy countenance. The two faces will be linked to one another for the rest of my days. Every time I imagine the one, the other appears and drives it away. And then, there is the terrible moment when I see the two faces superimposed upon one another. A Vilmafagu or a Faguvilma. Everything becomes distorted and vague. The faces are mutilated and lack expression. Death and decomposition could not do more to disfigure a face. Sometimes, though not very often, this vision tortures me in my sleep and makes me painfully aware that I will never be able to drive it away. Bathed in sweat, I wake up, my heart almost bursting in my breast. Then, transfixed under the spell of the nightmare, I spend all day hanging out at the café. Things only get moving after the first double cognac, which seems to act as a lubricant, making its way through my blood vessels to my brain and greasing the rusty shell of my subcortex. Then things start to happen. More glasses follow and precipitate my lethargic liberation. But it is still too early. The movement stops there. Most of Vilma's mouth and her closed lips remain stuck between Fagu's teeth. Her nose shifts a bit, her eyes, too, and then the contours of her face. From experience I know that after the first glass, half of Vilma's face is still covered by half of Fagu's face, while the other halves are free. I have to be quick with the next glass because I cannot bear this part of the vision. Once the third double is down the hatch, the two faces hardly touch one another and, by the fourth, they are completely separated. I need a fifth for Fagu's scowling face to disappear and, finally, to be alone with Vilma.

There she is, behind the bars of the wrought-iron fence. She is wearing that white dress, a belt around her waist, and with waves of her long hair flowing down over her shoulders. She is blonde so, in the sun, her hair shines like the golden fleece. I am quite sure that her dress is made of the same material as bridal gowns. The plan I conceived to take revenge upon Xhoda was not to kidnap her and make her my bride, although, dressed as she was, she looked very much like one. I stared at her with the eyes of a common thug, someone with criminal intent on his mind. What my exact intent was, I will reveal later. First of all, though, I must make clear something which all the guys of my generation in town knew, that whole pack of twelve- and thirteen-year-old rascals: Vilma belonged to Fagu. As such, she was closely watched over by his gang, who were among the toughest kids at school. Vilma was aware of this, too. She was twelve, as I was. Fagu was thirteen, a whole year older.

I cannot say what opinion Vilma had of the status she had been accorded by the others. I never really thought much about it. There was a convention which I accepted, as did everyone of my age, playfully learning the mommy-daddy game, that every boy should have a girl. For my part, I was reserved and did not take a role. Actually, I thought they were all crazy and that it was undignified for a boy to spend his time in the company of girls. If Fagu wanted to carry on playing that ridiculous mommy-daddy charade with Vilma, it was his affair. I regarded him as compromised and was surprised that all that gang of ruffians at school should accept Fagu as their leader. To put it briefly, Vilma would not have entered my life to that extent and in such a manner had I not seized upon the idea of taking revenge on Xhoda.

I often tried to convince myself that it was all a game of coincidence, of fatality, but alas, like everyone else in my generation, I was raised without religious education. I have heard say that religious people take comfort and find peace of mind in expressions such as "thus it was written." A religious person believes in a predetermined fate. But how was I, who believed in nothing, to find consolation? I do not think that the wicked will expiate their evil deeds in the flames of hell, nor do I believe that those who are good will be compensated in heaven. I would, however, like to believe that there is something like a last judgment. I cling to this ephemeral hope, for it is the only thing that keeps me going in the unending futility of my existence.

I soon realized that taking revenge on Xhoda would not be easy. Initially, I considered smashing the windows at his house, a freestanding building a distance away from the center of town and surrounded by a high wrought-iron fence laden with plants and creeping vines. There was an alley nearby and it was from there that I could shatter all the glass in the windows. I abandoned the idea, however. During the day, it was impossible to act without being noticed due to all the passersby, and I was afraid to go out at nighttime because the town was infested with packs of wild dogs. I also gave up the idea of hiding a snake in the drawer of the principal's desk, not because it was impossible to find a snake—the gypsies who lived down by the river would have caught one for me anytime—but, first, it was virtually impossible to get into the office, and second, it was even more impossible to get the drawer of his desk open. Three such attempts had been made at school and all of them had failed. I would therefore have to come up with some other method of taking revenge. And I did.

I happened upon the idea quite by coincidence. One day, in the schoolyard where Fagu's gang had gathered, I witnessed a scene which was nothing particular in itself. Fagu was beating up a boy who lived down by the river, while the members of his gang were looking on. All the other boys were watching the scene from a distance and everything was taking place in silence. The gypsy boy put up with the thrashing without saying a word until Fagu had had his fill and let him go, giving him a final kick in the ass. It was unthinkable that anyone would come to the aid of a gypsy. He was a stubby, apathetic lad, one of the few children from the riverside who attended school regularly. His name was Sherif and he was in the fifth grade, in class A, whereas I was in class C. I knew something else about him that was important. His father, a stubby gypsy, as apathetic as his son, was given the task at various times of the year of exterminating the wild dogs. It was said that if he did not do it, the dogs would overrun and destroy the whole town. To this end, he utilized pieces of poisoned beef liver, which had an immediate effect.

The bell rang and recess was over. The schoolyard behind the building emptied. Sherif remained alone in a corner. I am not sure what moved me to go over and speak to him. Either I pitied him or I just despised Fagu. And I definitely did despise Fagu. He was a brutal braggart. At any rate, I learned something I would not forget. Fagu had beaten Sherif up because the latter had teased Vilma in class the day before, and she had complained to Fagu. What a beast she was, just like her father! In fact, all three of them were beasts—her hench-man father, Vilma, and that street tough who debased himself all the more by giving in to her whims. It did not take much convincing to make Sherif my accomplice.

I played the game with exemplary hypocrisy.

I stress the word *hypocrisy*. At the time, I did not know what the word meant, but sometime at that age, hypocrisy got under my skin and into my blood. If someone had explained it to me, I would per-haps not have become the way I did. But no one explained it to me. From the first grade at school we had had lessons in moral education, yet I do not remember any teacher ever explaining the meaning of hypocrisy to us. I do recall something else—that the teachers acted differently in the presence of the principal than they did when he was not around. They often lied blatantly to him in our presence, but none of us said a word. We hated Xhoda as much as we feared him. We felt much the same way about the teachers. I had noticed that whenever a school inspector turned up, the principal would act peculiarly. He was kinder and more polite, and lied to the inspector, just as the teachers lied to him. And things turned out all right for him. We were raised to believe that we were the happiest children on earth. That was what the songs we learned taught us.

I, nonetheless, had reason to doubt whether we were indeed the happiest children on earth. I cannot speak for the others, but at home, I often witnessed scenes between my parents which were so violent that they would send shivers down my spine. To avert any misunderstanding, I must note that my father had no particular vices. He did not indulge in alcohol or tobacco, and I am convinced that he was not much of a ladies' man. It was my mother who wore the pants in our family. Father was head of the bookkeeping division at work, and Mother was a seamstress. I knew they tried not to fight in my presence, but they did not always succeed. What surprised me on most occasions was that the disputes were set off by completely insignificant matters. I would never have fought with my friends over such absurdities. Anyway, the storm clouds would gather, bringing with them insults, accusations, and counteraccusations. The first to grow weary of the disputes was my father. Deprived of a worthy opponent, my mother would sniff in defiance and calm down, too.

FROM THE LOSER

33

Then, when the room was bathed in a deafening silence, I would hear my father lament: "God, what a dog's life!" I thus concluded that one could not live as the happiest child on earth, as we were told in the songs we learned, and at the same time live a dog's life, as my father declared. This conclusion of mine confused me to no end and brought me face to face with another curious phenomenon—the theatrical talents of my parents. It is difficult for me to speak about this, but it is true. My parents were consummate actors.

There was a certain fellow named Hulusi, who lived in our apartment building. He is dead now. He was a short fellow and used to come around quite often. I remember that he could consume an enormous amount and it often happened that he would not budge until he had downed a whole bottle of raki. From the way my parents talked about him, I was of the impression that, at the first possible moment, they would seize him and throw him out the window. That is what I heard my father say at any rate. But the scene that I had long waited to witness and believed would take place, that is, my father chucking Hulusi, half his size, out the window, never happened. I waited eagerly for my father to seize Hulusi by the neck the moment he entered the room, and yet my father and mother beamed hospitably at his presence. Hulusi helped himself to the raki and stayed as long as he wanted. As soon as he was gone, the smiling masks on my parents' faces vanished. Father stuck his fists into his pockets and began to pace up and down the room like a tiger. Mother fell silent. Hulusi, so despised and looked down upon as he was, turned out to be our family's guardian angel. Without his assistance, my sister would never have been able to attend the teacher training college and, later, I would never have had a chance to go to college. But I did not know that at the time. I was not aware that our neighbor, Hulusi, who lived one floor above us, was the real power behind the throne in our town. Nor was I aware that to gain the good graces of our guardian angel, my parents had to pay eternal tribute—the loss of their dignity. There were many other things I did not know, things which life would later teach me, one by one. In those years, my brain offered me a very simple and easy, indeed I would say conformist, explanation for all these great dilemmas—everyone around me was an actor, both my teachers and my parents. They would don and remove their masks whenever it suited them. Accordingly,

I would have to find masks of my own, just as the grown-ups had. This was the definitive solution to the quandary. Concerning the dilemma as to whether we were the happiest children on earth, I had come up with an explanation which one might even call original. We were and were not. It was like the mangy dogs roaming around town. I could not conceive of these animals being happy. They got kicked around wherever they went, not to mention the poisoned liver which Sherif's father set out for them. Pet dogs, on the other hand (most families with houses and gardens kept a dog), in particular lapdogs, I considered to be the happiest species on earth. Even Vilma had a lapdog. It was white and had curly hair.

Vilma was the apple of Xhoda's eye. The lapdog was the apple of Vilma's eye. I decided to poison Vilma's dog.

■ □ ■ □ ■

THE SLOGANS IN STONE

Ylljet Aliçka

IT WAS IMMEDIATELY AFTER ANDREA FINISHED HIS STUDIES THAT HE
received an appointment as a schoolteacher in an isolated mountain
village in the north.

His father accompanied him in silence to the train station. At the
moment they were to part, hardly holding back his tears, he said
to him, "Work hard, take good care of yourself, and pay attention,
because life's not easy."

He arrived at the mountain village that evening. The school was
small, a mere ten teachers, six of whom were from the nearby town.
One of them was from the capital.

The next day, the oldest of the schoolteachers, Pashk, willingly accepted the task of explaining to him "how to work and live so as not
to get into conflict with anyone else."

Pashk began by depicting the hierarchy of the village authorities.
First of all, there was the Party Secretary, the teacher Sabaf, and then
the chairman of the agricultural cooperative. When he finally got
around to mentioning the school principal, he characterized him as
follows: "He's not a bad guy. He doesn't beat the pupils very often, but
when he does, he beats them until he's out of breath. Try to keep on
good terms with him because everything is in his hands . . . everything
from your teaching schedule to the slogans."

"What slogans?" interrupted Andrea.

"What do you mean, what slogans?" uttered Pashk, astonished. "Every teacher and his class are assigned a slogan in stone for which they are responsible all the time."

"I see," said Andrea.

"You think it's no great matter at all, do you?" he asked.

"No, no, not in the least," responded Andrea, attentively.

The surprised expression on Andrea's face forced Pashk to explain a few things which he would never have imagined that people did not know.

"Well, since you're new here as a teacher and have your career ahead of you, let me be frank with you. If you want to be respected by the Party and the authorities, roll up your sleeves and take good care of your slogan.

"To take care of your slogan, you have to be systematic," he continued, "and never neglect it. What I mean is you have to go out and check on it at least once a week. If it rains, the slogan's appearance will suffer. The rain cuts furrows into the soil and can cover the letters over with mud. It dilutes the whitewash and the stones look blotched. You know what happened here recently?"

"No," replied Andrea.

"Well, how could you?" Pashk recalled. "It took a full six months to find out beyond any doubt how Baft's slogan became damaged. To tell you the truth, the teacher Baft had been reputed for his excellent slogans. But a few months ago, all of a sudden, his slogan began to deteriorate. If you were looking for Baft, you knew where to find him. He was always out at his slogan fixing the letters. He spent more and more time there, even in the evenings.

"The truth is that when a shepherd from the cooperative, a member of one of the most bourgeois, déclassé families in the village, took his sheep out to pasture early in the morning, he cast a spell on that teacher's slogan." Pashk's eyes took on the air of an investigator. "Poor Baft was exhausted, going out every day to fix his slogan. He was constantly moaning and groaning, 'Why am I having all this bad luck? Why do the sheep keep grazing on my slogan?' He could not imagine what in his slogan, THE MOST DANGEROUS FOE IS A FOE FORGOTTEN, had attracted the sheep in the first place and caused them to destroy it.

"Baft asked the principal several times to change his slogan, 'just because I'm superstitious,' but the principal was in no mood to do so.

"In fact, Baft himself was the first person to cast doubts on the 'guilt' of the sheep. After having studied the terrain, he expressed his doubts to the Party Secretary. 'It's odd,' he had explained. 'There are lots of other sheep paths in the area of my slogan, much easier ones, and after all, sheep are not particularly well known for their bravery, as, for example, are goats, who will scamper up any steep hillside, like the one where my slogan is located, despite the danger.'

"Then another clue assisted them in their investigation of the case when it became known that the village shepherd had recently been buying particularly large amounts of salt at the shop.

"The shepherd was obviously up to something. With handfuls of salt he got the sheep to lick off the word FOE. You know, of course, that sheep go mad for salt. So his suspicions turned out to be true. The local secret police officer was informed immediately. A whole group of volunteers was then called up to guard Baft's slogan day and night. Just imagine, the villagers hid among the bushes and waited for hours for the shepherd's sheep to pass by. In the end, the whole affair was uncovered. It was early in the morning when the guards, or rather the villagers, observed the sheep of the cooperative destroying the very letters which Baft and his pupils had arranged with such great effort. Having ascertained the facts, the villagers pounced, probably upon a signal given by the secret police officer.

"When he was detained, the shepherd of course denied everything. It was only two or three days later that he revealed his true colors and was arrested for hostile activities. He tried to defend himself up to the very last moment, claiming that he was innocent because there were only hoofprints there and because sheep were not responsible before the law or any other such nonsense.

"The principal later changed Baft's slogan and gave him another hill. He assigned him one of those slogans with a GLORY TO or a PRAISE BE, which require less maintenance and are always in fashion.

"In the final analysis, what matters to a teacher is not what the slogan says, but the number of letters. From the moment he gets it, he instinctively starts counting the letters. . . ."

It was with the history of Baft that Pashk terminated his account of Andrea's coming teaching career.

Two days later, Andrea was called to the principal's office to be given his class, his teaching schedule, and other necessities. When it came to the slogan, the principal pondered, "Because you are new here, I'll give you a site not too far from the school building, and for your slogan, well. . . ." The director opened his red notebook, hesitated, and then added, "Actually, you can have your choice. There are two left over at the moment. One is THE PARTY IS THE TIP OF THE SWORD OF THE WORKING CLASS, and the other one is . . . is CHROMIUM BREAKS THROUGH THE BLOCKADE." Andrea, who now knew all about the slogans, replied with a note of hesitation in his voice, "I'll take the one about chromium."

"All right," said the absentminded principal. "It won't be too difficult for you. Frrok had that site before, so the ground will already have been leveled. But Frrok, who was getting close to retirement, used to tend to his slogan less and less. You know, old age. . . . Anyway, take that one. I hope you won't have any trouble," he added in closing.

The next day, after class, Andrea took his pupils out. They walked for about half an hour up to the site of his slogan. The site had indeed been leveled, but the existing slogan was in a sorry state. There was, at any rate, enough room for the new one.

There was great commotion among the pupils when the time came to distribute the individual letters. Calculating the number of stones needed for each letter, they all tried to get the letters which caused the least work. There was great shouting at the start to get an *l*, of which there happened to be only one, then an *o*, and then a *u*, and so forth.

Confused by all the hubbub and wanting to be as exact as possible in his distribution of the letters, Andrea remembered to ask, "How did your teacher Frrok used to divide them?"

"Oh, he changed the system quite often. At the start he did it by alphabetical order, then the girls got to choose first, and then the sick children were given only the dots on the *i*'s or a comma."

"But Frrok took sides and had his favorite pupils," another pupil was heard to say.

"All right then, we'll continue this time the way we started out . . . and I am going to take a letter, too," uttered Andrea enthusiastically.

"No, no, teacher!" shouted the pupils in protest. "You just supervise."

Everything went smoothly after that. For about three hours they rummaged around like squirrels, collecting stones from the bushes.

When they were finished, the pupils themselves thought that their slogan had turned out quite well.

All tired by now, they set off one by one in various directions with their backpacks and tools over their shoulders and shouted to him, "Have a good lunch, Teacher!"

He felt sorry for them as he watched them leave. They had little to eat, were poorly dressed, but nonetheless they were happy kids. None of them understood or even attempted to understand what the slogan meant.

Slowly he returned to his room. He was weary but with the knowledge and tranquillity of mind that he had fulfilled his duties well. He lay down and right away fell into a profound sleep.

He met the other teachers when he woke up. None of them talked about the slogans. He observed them, all of them with their jackets draped over their arms, cigarettes in the corners of their mouths, with their quiet, almost shepherdlike manner, as they set off, saying, "I'm just going out to have a look at my slogan."

It had become a real pastime for them.

"What else is there to do here in the middle of nowhere?" Andrea often thought to himself.

Later, he also got used to going out to have a look at his slogan, at least once a week. He would clean it up, remove all the leaves, dirt, and mud, adjust one or two of the letters, sit and rest among them, and greet the farmers who were returning from their labors.

But when five months had passed, Andrea's slogan was changed. In fact, most of the slogans were changed.

Pashk had explained to him that changes in the slogans occurred only rarely, and it was at any rate the Central Committee of the Party which authorized such changes, on the basis of several exceptionally strict criteria. A number of factors were taken into account for the distribution of new slogans: the political spectrum of the district, zone, or countryside in question; the percentage of kulaks, deportees, political prisoners, and common prisoners; the number of Communist Party members; the economic development of the zone; harvest yields; the rate of success against adverse weather conditions; local cultural and historical traditions; and the specific situation of the zone in question. For example, it was said that once, when a school principal was caught in flagrante delicto with a female teacher of questionable political origins, they immediately changed all the slogans in the zone. LONG LIVE PROLETARIAN INTERNATIONALISM, for instance, was replaced by VIGILANCE, VIGILANCE, AND YET MORE VIGILANCE and by LET US RAISE THE STANDARDS OF PROLETARIAN MORALS.

The distribution of slogans was usually the last point on the agenda of the teachers' council meeting, but the teachers normally knew in advance whether or not to expect a new distribution. The day before the meeting, Sabaf, the Party Secretary, would be called to the Central Committee, and when he got back, he would behave very solemnly, acutely aware of the gravity of the political situation. He seemed to know just how curious the teachers were to find out as quickly as possible what their new slogans would be. He would nod left and right, giving an indifferent greeting. It was during those days that the teachers would often treat Sabaf to food and drinks.

Many of them envied Sabaf on such occasions.

The principal argued that the slogans had to be changed because of the coming visit by a politburo member to a northern town, noting that the official in question might use the road that passed by their village.

Emotion and impatience prevailed at the moment the slogans were to be distributed. Their contents and lengths were interpreted in many ways. They were seen as a sign of sympathy or antipathy by the ruling Party organs.

The principal quietly began reading out the names of the teachers and then the slogans. Discreet moans of anguish or sighs of relief could be heard from time to time in the classroom.

A stir was caused by the slogan given to Diana, the teacher from the capital, whom Andrea did not know well. They had talked a couple of times while hitchhiking, but since the drivers always preferred to take girls with them, it often happened that Andrea got left behind and had to wait quite some time to get a lift, or didn't get a lift at all. On such occasions, he would return to his room and would spend all of the following day at his slogan.

For reasons which were not entirely clear, the principal seemed to dislike Diana. That became apparent when he assigned her the mile-long slogan WE SHALL TAKE TO THE HILLS AND TO THE MOUNTAINS AND MAKE THEM AS FERTILE AS THE PLAINS. This time, he gave her a slogan with no less than forty-seven letters: LET US THINK, LET US WORK, LET US LIVE LIKE REVOLUTIONARIES. The corner of Diana's lower lip began to quiver with anger. She tried to preserve her composure but was unable to do so and finally burst into tears with, "I knew it, I knew it from the very start!"

"What did you know from the very start?" asked the principal frigidly.

"Please, Comrade Principal, how long are you going to continue doing this to me? It is not fair of you to take your personal likes and dislikes out on people by means of the slogans."

The anger in her voice was more than apparent. The teachers' council froze on the spot. No one dared to speak.

The principal continued to speak as if nothing had happened. "I don't understand. I really don't understand. What do you mean by dislikes? Or have you perhaps got something against the slogan? This is the slogan which Comrade Enver Hoxha used himself during the Seventh Party Congress," he added, with a sly gleam in his eye.

His words dropped like a bomb. Though she was unable to conceal her anger, Diana did not have the courage to say another word. Discreet glances of sympathy were cast in her direction. Gjin, one of the more affable teachers in the group, broke the silence. Though his hands and his voice were trembling, Gjin made the principal a proposal to calm the situation down.

"Comrade Principal," he suggested, "may I swap my slogan FULL SPEED AHEAD with Diana's?"

But the principal would have none of it. "No, of course not! We are not going to spend all day here redistributing slogans to make everyone happy. They are our political duty, and if anyone is opposed to that, well, that's a different matter," he concluded.

While leaving the meeting, Andrea heard Gjin whisper to Diana, "Don't worry, Diana. Don't get so upset about it. I'll do your slogan for you. What will it cost me after all? Only a couple of days of leave. Or we'll go out one day and do it together. All right?"

But Diana was in such a state that she could hear nothing.

"She is really quite attractive," Andrea said to himself as he watched her frowning.

This time, Andrea received the slogan THE STRONGER THE DICTATORSHIP OF THE PROLETARIAT, THE STRONGER OUR SOCIALIST

DEMOCRACY. He was not upset by its length, and indeed, when he was finished, the principal commended him on its orderly layout: "Andrea, I have a very good impression of your slogan. Congratulations!"

"Thank you," replied Andrea in satisfaction.

Two years passed with the same slogan. He would go out to have a look at his slogan as usual. Whenever he was not able to return home for the weekend or when he was lonely, it seemed to be his salvation. "Thank God I've got the slogan. What else would I do here in the middle of nowhere if I didn't have it?" he often pondered as he cleaned it, stroking the stones fondly.

One autumn afternoon, while he was smoking a cigarette all by himself, he met Diana in the empty school yard.

"What's up?" he asked.

"Nothing special," she replied.

"Nice weather," he noted.

"Yes."

"Shall we go for a walk out to the slogans?"

"Why bother?" she said. "There hasn't been any rain for quite a while."

"What about the leaves? The autumn leaves might have covered them over. But whatever you want."

"All right," said Diana, showing no particular interest.

Slowly they set off through the woods.

When they got to the brook where the path divides, Diana dipped her hands in the water, washed her face, and moistened her hair. Then, taking another scoop of water, she sprinkled Andrea with it. He was confused and Diana laughed loudly. He soon recovered though and gave her the same back. She splashed him this time and ran off. There was no sense in Andrea's standing there like a wet fool. He took courage, filled his hands with water, and ran after her. He overtook her beside a tree and, while catching his breath, threw the water over her shoulder. The water flowed down her dress, making parts of it stick to her body. Andrea could hold back no longer. He threw his arms around her and hugged her like a child.

But Diana withdrew from his embrace, saying, "No!"

"Why not?" asked Andrea, still breathing heavily.

"Because I don't want to," declared Diana and walked slowly toward the hill where her slogan was located.

THE SLOGANS IN STONE

"But why did you spray me with water if you didn't want to?" wondered Andrea, setting off for his own slogan. When he got there, he found it in good order. The stones were still covered by the fresh coat of whitewash. Here and there, a few leaves had fallen on them. He cleaned them up and, not knowing what else to do, headed up the hill to see what Diana was doing.

He was surprised to find her sitting on the grass beside her slogan, LET US THINK, LET US WORK, LET US LIVE LIKE REVOLUTIONARIES, covered in leaves from the surrounding trees.

She looked completely lost. Her dress was still wet.

He sat down beside her and stammered in a somewhat sheepish fashion, "Sorry."

"Sorry for what?" she asked.

"For a while ago."

"No problem. I had almost forgotten."

Silence once again.

"Why don't you clean up the leaves?" Andrea inquired.

"I like it better the way it is, draped in autumn leaves, better than all that white like a hospital. It's more romantic this way, don't you think?" said Diana, who seemed to be talking to herself. "It seems to carry a different message this way somehow, more of a romantic revolutionary slogan."

"Revolutionary romanticism . . . ," added Andrea with a smile.

"You should still clean it up," added Andrea, who stood up and began to brush all the leaves off her long slogan.

Diana studied him. She then got up herself, approached, picked up a leaf, and as she was about to throw it away, gently took hold of his hand. He said nothing and continued working with his head bowed.

She squeezed his hand and looked him in the eyes. She then took his head in her hands and, pulling him toward her, gave him a sudden kiss.

In no time at all, they were lying on the soft earth between the words LIKE and REVOLUTIONARIES. Neither of them noticed that the careless movement of their legs had toppled one of the letters in REVOLUTIONARIES.

They returned to the village late that evening.

The next morning, they greeted one another calmly, as if nothing had happened at all. From that day on, they went out to the slogans more often.

The monotony of village life was interrupted by something that happened to one of the elder teachers, Llesh. He taught at a little one-room school which served as an annex to the main school but was a member of the teaching staff like Andrea. Llesh's school was two hours away from the center of the cooperative. According to regulations, the principal had to inspect it two times a year, but because it was quite a distance to walk, he rarely went.

The misfortune occurred when, on his last inspection, the principal was surprised to discover the slogan VIETNAM WILL BE VICTORIOUS discreetly located in a ravine right near Llesh's school.

The principal was flabbergasted. The Vietnam War had been over for fifteen years. In addition, the slogan was in an excellent state, having been daubed with a fresh coat of whitewash. The principal did not know what to do. He liked Llesh, in particular because they played chess together. Llesh was known among the staff members as a devoted teacher and not the sort of person who would indulge in such jokes. But the principal wanted to be on the safe side. He might have been accused subsequently of not having taken action. As such, at the next staff meeting he brought up the issue of Llesh's slogan as the last point on the agenda.

Llesh had arrived two hours before the meeting started. He was as pale as wax, a sorry state indeed, as he put out one cigarette after the other, endeavoring to act as quiet and friendly as possible with the other teachers.

He addressed them out in the school yard, "Hey, guys, we haven't played for quite a while. What about a game of chess, a teachers' championship?"

Pashk took pity on him and said, "Look, Llesh, this is not the right moment for chess."

"You know what? I'll beat the pants off you, Pashk, if we play against one another," Llesh said, giving a laugh.

None of the other teachers smiled.

During the meeting, before they got to the issue of the Vietnam slogan, one could hear Llesh's knee thumping nervously under the desk where he was sitting. It was a difficult moment for him. He was used to hearing praise for his good work. This time, things were different.

The principal, however, treated the problem very briefly. He seemed to want to skim over it in a formal manner. He stated the facts of the case and turned to Llesh, inquiring, "Tell us, Llesh, how did all this come about?"

Llesh was unnerved and confused by the question.

"How did what come about?"

There was a long silence. Llesh then rose to his feet and, with a few awkward movements, began searching through his pockets. All the others watched him attentively. Finally, he extracted a crumpled piece of paper. It was clear to everyone that he had prepared a written statement.

He looked at the piece of paper but, for a while, did not manage to say a word. Confused as he was, he did not realize that he was holding the paper the wrong way around. Gjin, who was sitting beside him, whispered, "Look, Llesh, you've got it upside down."

"Oh," stammered Llesh with a sigh of relief. "Thank you, Gjin," he continued with evident gratitude and, glancing around at the staff, began, "Comrades . . . "

Before he could say another word, the principal interrupted him, "Don't bother, Llesh. There is no need for a long discussion of the matter. Just tell us about the slogan. . . ."

Poor Llesh was really mixed up now. You could see from the dark circles under his eyes that he had spent a lot of time preparing his paper. But his colleagues were of the opinion that the matter should be dealt with as briefly as possible. Mixing up his words from the very start, Llesh thus endeavored to explain concisely what had "come about."

Some seventeen years earlier, a particularly zealous Party Secretary called Nik had insisted that slogans be built everywhere, even in the most remote villages. "Wherever we are able," he had stated, "on sites which can be well seen and even on sites which cannot be seen at all." Llesh had received the slogan about Vietnam and had completed it according to the technical specifications he had received. Of course, later on, everyone else had forgotten Llesh's slogan. No one ever told him not to keep the slogan in good condition, so he continued to go out every week after class, sometimes with the pupils and sometimes on his own, to see that everything was in order.

"OK, but why Vietnam? Vietnam was liberated fifteen years ago!" asked Sabaf.

"But that's the slogan they gave me," Llesh replied innocently. "And let me say it again, no one told me not to keep it up."

There was no point in going on any further. The only thing Llesh could be accused of was an eminent lack of knowledge of current events.

"After all, what else can you expect from the place he lives in?" Pashk whispered in Andrea's ear.

But when the principal, concluding the matter, referred in passing to Llesh's failings, in particular for not having taken "appropriate measures to keep up with the international situation," Llesh reacted immediately, saying, "As far as I am aware, Vietnam was and still is subject to the aggressive designs of the capitalist countries."

"Yes, of course," replied the principal, obviously regretting that he had broached the subject in the first place. "Llesh, go and dismantle the slogan and let's put an end to the matter."

The teachers all nodded in approval and were beginning to collect their briefcases to depart. But Llesh, certain now that the initial danger had passed, would not give up that easily. "If you would allow me to continue, Comrade Principal?" Without waiting for a reply, he rose to his feet, full of self-confidence, and continued, "Comrades, I have endeavored to carry out my duties to the best of my abilities, to construct a proper slogan and . . . "

"Yes, of course, Llesh," noted with principal, showing signs of losing his patience. "No one here has questioned your sense of responsibility and no one will condemn you for dismantling the slogan. The only problem was that it is fifteen years old and is now out of date."

"All right," noted Llesh, not to be outdone, "then give me one of the modern slogans."

"What do you want me to give you?" asked the principal nervously. "What do you want out there in the middle of nowhere?"

Llesh, believing that the principal had asked him seriously about what slogan he wanted, stated in a faint voice, "I'd like the one YANKEES, HANDS OFF VIETNAM."

There was a long "ooh" of amazement and impatience among the other teachers.

Sensing that the official character of the meeting was being lost, the principal concluded sharply with the words, "Comrades, having dealt with all the issues at hand, we shall now adjourn the meeting. I wish you all a pleasant evening."

The teachers all rose to make a speedy exit. Llesh was the last to leave. In silence, he lit a cigarette and, taking a deep puff, said to himself, "I lost out."

The news that Llesh had been deprived of his slogan spread quickly in the village.

His wife, Maria, kept to herself in the brigade. When a number of days had passed, one of her colleagues inquired sympathetically, "Maria, is it true what people are saying in the village?"

"What do you mean?" replied Maria coolly.

"Well, we heard that your husband, Llesh . . . I mean . . . I hope you don't mind . . . that they took away his slogan. What I mean is, he doesn't have a slogan anymore."

Maria bowed her head in shame and gave a nod. "Yes, it's true," she replied. "To tell you the truth, I'm not worried about the slogan but about Llesh. We are going through a difficult phase. My husband has lost his appetite and can't sleep well anymore. You know, he really cared more for that slogan than he did for his own children."

The other women in the brigade tried to comfort her.

"Don't worry. It's no great disaster. Let him dismantle the slogan about that country. What was the name again? He'll be all right for a while without a slogan until the people in the village have forgotten the matter. Then he can always make an application for a new one."

"Thanks for your kind words," said Maria, "but the problem is that Llesh is lost without it. He is really on edge. He's not used to criticism at work. The affair with the slogan about Vietnam has really affected him deeply."

The woman then gave Maria an idea which surprised not only her but the whole brigade. "If the situation is really that bad, why don't you get him to build a slogan on your fence at home? You don't need permission. You could even use the one about Vietnam, or something else, and then everything would be all right. Your children are already old enough and could help you keep it in order."

Maria was speechless at the thought.

"My Llesh doesn't need anyone's help. He can do it himself, but I don't really know if he will agree to do it without permission."

"Why shouldn't he?" insisted the others.

No one ever found out whether he had accepted the suggestion of his wife's brigade, but one thing was for sure: he never again applied for another slogan.

Less than two weeks had passed since the meeting when the principal and Sabaf summoned Andrea to the office. Placing his arm over Andrea's shoulder, the principal said, "Andrea, I would like to give you something special this time. When you drive up to the top of the hill, you know the ugly wall of the warehouse you can see from there? It looks so empty. That's why Sabaf and I thought it would be a good idea to cover it with a long slogan in red paint." Sabaf nodded in approval. "The school children can't manage, so you'll have to do it yourself. We'll get you a ladder, a brush, and some paint. The slogan is LONG LIVE THE DICTATORSHIP OF THE PROLETARIAT."

Andrea accepted willingly. Before he left the office, he turned to the principal and asked, "Excuse me, but what color did you want for the slogan?"

The principal gave a chuckle and, looking at Sabaf, replied: "But that's obvious, isn't it, Andrea? It has to be red."

The warehouse was an old building in a terrible state of disrepair. It was gray, dusty, and had been built of large, heavy, and irregular blocks of stone in uneven rows. Andrea did not go back home that weekend. Instead, he began Saturday afternoon by taking measurements for the slogan and worked all day Sunday on it. He couldn't find any paint in the warehouse itself, so he began with an anticorrosive agent. The work was exhausting. He had not anticipated the difficulties involved. The paint seeped into the cracks in the wall, the letters ruptured all over the stone facade, and the remaining plaster crumbled into bits every time the paintbrush passed over it. It took two whole days of work.

"How are you getting along, Teacher?" asked the villagers from time to time. "It looks really nice!"

"Thanks," he replied politely from the top of the ladder and continued putting great effort into the work, covered as he was in the anticorrosive paint and dust.

Marta, the head of the corn harvest brigade, who was quite a ripe beauty of her own, teased him, "Careful with your hands, Andrea. The paint will stain them and eat at your skin. What are all the girls in the big city going to think about that?"

Andrea gave a hearty laugh.

When he finally finished the job late in the evening, he wasn't happy with the slogan at all. He knew how to build one on the hillside, knew how to even out the terrain, but he was no good at a wall slogan.

He returned home late that night, completely dissatisfied with his work. And rightly so.

Two days later, the principal and Sabaf summoned him urgently to the office. He sensed that something unpleasant was about to happen.

"What the hell have you been doing up there, Andrea? You have no idea how many people are upset!" exclaimed the principal, who was known to be extremely vicious when he was in trouble.

"Why? What's wrong?" Andrea managed to stammer in a faint voice.

"What do you mean, why?" The principal, being studied by Sabaf, did not know what to do to appear really upset. "What did you write the slogan with? Your hands or your feet?" The principal glanced at Sabaf from the corner of his eye as if to say, "Should we keep our mouths shut this time, too?"

But the expression on Sabaf's face betrayed nothing. The matter was obviously to be taken seriously.

Andrea endeavored to find out what was going on. They informed him later. The District Party Secretary for Propaganda had arrived for an inspection. After having briefly checked all the slogans in stone, his glance fell upon the slogan on the warehouse. He approached it and spent a full five minutes staring at it in silence. He then turned to Sabaf, asking, "Who wrote that?"

"Andrea. He teaches science and comes from the capital, Comrade Secretary," Sabaf replied promptly.

The Secretary then set off for the offices of the cooperative without saying another word. Everyone in his retinue thought he had forgotten the matter, but the moment he was about to enter the Party office, he turned to the group and, after a ponderous moment of silence, stated briefly, "The slogan has been written without requisite devotion to duty."

The message of the Party Secretary was eminently clear.

Two days later, Andrea was summoned to a meeting of the Party.

It had been two days of great solitude for him. The other teachers were reserved and Sabaf had not spoken to him at all.

The main accusation made against him at the meeting came from Sabaf, who, endeavoring to find an expression which was both one of principle and one which would hit hard, opened the session as follows:

"Comrade Andrea, the Party organization would like to know the reasons, or rather, the real motives which caused you, or should I say, instigated you to write, or more precisely, to botch up the slogan with LONG LIVE THE DICTATORSHIP OF DE PLORETARIAT? To put it more bluntly, I would like you to explain frankly to the meeting exactly who put you up to this."

The atmosphere was tense indeed.

Among the arguments which Andrea presented in his explanation were the bad quality of the stone, the filthiness of the warehouse wall, the old plaster. . . .

"Come on, come on now," interrupted Sabaf abruptly, "if you keep on talking about the stones and the plaster, we will get nowhere."

"But what else could it be, Comrade Sabaf?" asked Andrea confusedly.

"I can tell you," he replied, "but it would be in your best interests to tell us yourself. Listen, my good man, the Party has no time to deal with matters of such insignificance. I was hoping you would open your heart to the organization and justify your actions, presenting due self-criticism, but as far as I can see here, this does not seem to be the case. As such, comrades," continued Sabaf, clearing his throat and enunciating more distinctly, "it would be insufficient to state simply that Andrea wrote the slogan without requisite devotion to duty, making it evident that he is not a great proponent of the dictatorship of the proletariat. No, comrades, the problem goes deeper than that." After a lengthy analysis of the principle of class struggle, he noted, "The principal reason is to be found in his family background, his relations. His paternal uncle committed suicide during the war, and his maternal uncle was sent into internal exile, so now he . . . Can't you see, my Communist comrades, what sly means the enemy has been using here? Yes, yes, the enemy of the working class. Can't you see how he has distanced himself from the Party, which made every attempt to extend a helping hand and get him out of the mire he has been wallowing in? But he refused to take it."

Andrea could not make any sense of what was going on. He did, however, realize that his life and his fate were at stake.

"Wait a moment, Comrade Sabaf," interrupted one of the elder Communists at the meeting, who was respected for his balanced opinions. "Let us not let things get out of hand here. I am not denying that this teacher has made a mistake but not to the extent that one could call him an enemy of the working class. I would therefore ask you to reconsider the matter more calmly."

Andrea had lost the thread of their conversation. He was then asked to leave the meeting room so that they could consider the matter and come to a decision. About an hour later, Sabaf came out and announced to him coolly and definitively, "The Party has decided this time to extend its hand to you. You will be given only six months of disciplinary work with the brigade."

"Thank you," replied Andrea blankly.

He was assigned to Marta's brigade. The villagers were reserved in their welcome. He worked hard, and when he returned home to his room late at night, he slept like a log.

From time to time, the villagers would ask him to read the newspaper to them.

Marta treated him well. She would often tease him about his delicate hands, "like those of a little baby."

One day, she approached while he was having lunch all alone during the break and said, "You'll be working this afternoon on the other plot, the one down at the bottom of the hill, and will be harvesting corn. If you want, I can help you."

"Thanks," said Andrea, touched by the gesture, "but there's no need. I can manage by myself."

"Oh . . . ," replied Marta with a laugh, "you don't want to work with me?"

Her imposing breasts heaved as she laughed. He stared at her with a twinkle in his eyes.

Later that afternoon, she found him harvesting among the tall sheaves of corn. She, too, began to strip the cobs of their foliage. Suddenly, without speaking a single word, they united and were rolling on the ground. It started to rain and they found themselves covered in mud.

Night was quickly falling when they parted, each of them stealing home along different paths through the cornfield. The hounds could be heard barking in the distance.

Drenched, he returned to his room.

When the six months with the brigade were over, Andrea resumed his activities at the school where he had been teaching. The principal welcomed him back as if nothing had happened. He gave him a new slogan and, upon leaving the room, noted, "Oh, I almost forgot. Listen, Andrea, some of the overzealous teachers have recently begun using white silicate blocks for their slogans instead of natural stone. They are obviously more attractive, but the practice has been condemned by the District Party Committee. It has also had a negative effect on the pupils. They have been caught stealing bricks from construction sites and coming to school with their backpacks over one shoulder and a bag of bricks over the other. And actually, when you compare them to those made of natural materials, the new slogans do lose something of the spontaneous character with which the masses express their own free views."

They looked one another in the eyes for a brief moment.

"I agree, Comrade Principal," replied Andrea politely. "I'll bear it in mind." As he left the office, he began counting the number of letters in his new slogan.

ADONIS

Ylljet Aliçka

MY FATHER PASSED AWAY IN JULY, OF PERFECTLY NATURAL CAUSES. AT his age—he was over eighty—any little thing is enough to kill you. In my father's case it was the heat wave that year, which did away with quite a number of people younger than he was.

Because it was so hot, the people who had come around to pay their respects advised me, not without good reason, not to leave my dead father in the house overnight up until the funeral the next day. "Put him somewhere freezing cold, because otherwise . . . " My distant cousin left the rest of her suggestion open. In fact, this very logical advice came as a surprise to me.

"Where am I supposed to put him?" I asked.

"What do you mean, where?" she replied. "You put him where the dead are supposed to be put—in the morgue."

"But," interrupted my stepmother, who had lived with my father for the last thirty years of his life, "how is the boy going to get into the . . . what do you call it . . . the morgue? I mean, how is he going to take the body? We have no idea about the regulations and don't know anyone there at all!"

The discussion did not last long because a doctor, who had arrived to pay his respects, recommended that I contact Adonis, the keeper at the morgue.

"It is only a question of one night," advised the doctor, "and it might be a good idea to give him a little something."

"Sure," I replied, relieved.

That evening, we lifted the coffin into a car which my employer had put at our disposal, and I drove off alone.

The morgue was a one-story building separated from the hospital. It had cream-colored walls and was patchy-looking from the fallen plaster. It was surrounded on all sides by weeds, most of which had withered in the heat. The windows were fortified with rusty iron bars. The only thing which added a hint of life to this dreary picture was Adonis.

Adonis was slouching around the grounds, smoking a cigarette. His stubby fingers were stained from tobacco or from the solution used to disinfect the corpses. I was surprised at the extent to which he resembled the rigors of his profession.

His unkempt hair rose vertically and his eyes were deeply entrenched in their sockets. He was thickset, had bushy eyebrows, and his white shirt was covered in yellowish stains. A jacket hung loosely from his shoulders and his trousers were misbuttoned.

I introduced myself and explained my problem to him.

He sighed and replied, "I have great respect for the doctor, but it is rather difficult to find room at the moment. Who is the deceased?" he continued, in a low, respectful voice.

"My father."

"Oh, I'm sorry to hear that," he went on in an official tone, "but, as I said, it is a real problem. We have been getting a lot of bodies over the last few days, not only from the hospital, but also from poor people like yourself."

I remembered what the doctor had told me and took out a five-thousand-lek banknote. The gesture did not go unnoticed, and Adonis hastened to add, "But we can give it a try. We'll find some solution."

"Thanks," I replied.

Adonis was right. It was very difficult to find a free space. He opened the freezer and began shuffling the bodies around. This he did in a quiet, reverent, almost ritual manner and noted earnestly, "I am not the type of person who likes to take money for nothing. I don't just pretend to freeze the bodies and then have them melt on you like ice before you get home. I am accustomed to doing my work properly. What I mean is, I freeze the bodies to perfection."

To prove his point, he again opened the freezer door and pulled out a wooden tray on which was lying the corpse of a young girl whose face was pale either from death or from being frozen.

Adonis grabbed the body by the shoulder and, suddenly, as if he were checking the ripeness of a watermelon, gave it a whack on the forehead with his hammer. There was a strange metallic vibration.

I was stunned. Adonis invited me to give her a whack, too.

"Go ahead, she won't bite you."

"No thanks, it's all right. It's obvious she's frozen. But, tell me, how did she die?"

"The girl? I'm not too sure. She probably committed suicide."

"Why?"

"How should I know?" he answered coolly and switched to his favorite subject. "The best thing is to clarify things from the beginning so that there are no problems. Your father is going to be as well frozen as this girl by tomorrow morning."

"I am quite convinced of that," I stated, hoping that the discussion could be brought to a swift conclusion.

"Bring your father on in," said Adonis in a resolute manner, once he had made room.

"Here's a spot for him," he added, pointing to a rusty freezer. It was not clear whether it had been cream-colored from the start or had paled with age. It contained three shelves.

"There's an old-age pensioner here that they brought in a week ago whom they still haven't picked up, and there's a woman they brought in this morning."

"That's all right," I said, and we loaded my father into the freezer. As I was closing the door, my eyes fell upon my father's hand. As a child, I used to stare at his hands when I was trying to get money out of him. He never refused me. He suffered his whole life long for having left me without a mother.

Touched by Adonis's kindness, I took another five-thousand-lek note out of my pocket and passed it to him without saying a word.

Lurching toward me with the expression of someone about to make a historic decision, he grinned and said: "You know what, lad? I'm really touched. Look, we are going to store your father in a special freezer. It's actually full, but we'll find a solution. What do you say?"

"I'm not sure. You know better than I do."

"One thing is certain," he added, "you freeze to the bone once you're in there. Your relatives wouldn't even recognize you."

I thanked him, not too eager to hear his detailed explanation.

He shuffled over and opened the special freezer. It had four shelves, all of which were occupied.

"I'll remove the one on the bottom. He's frozen solid. Not even a furnace could melt him," muttered Adonis, speaking more to himself than to me. "I'll then stick this other fellow on the bottom tray and . . ." He stored the second one on the bottom shelf and, having taken a deep breath, looked at me and said, "Or do you think I should move the agronomist they brought in yesterday and put him on the upper shelf so that it'll be easier to get him out tomorrow? Let's see. All right. Give me a hand, will you, and we'll shift the old-age pensioner. He's been here for a whole week and no one's given a thought to picking him up."

Within five minutes there were four bodies on the floor, spread out stiffly in different directions. Adonis lost his train of thought for a moment and turned to me:

"Where'll we put this one?" He was referring to the old-age pensioner.

"I really don't know," I hesitated, with a hint of guilt in my voice.

"All right, all right," he said. "I'll put him in with someone else. It's better to get 'em into the other fridge rather than leave 'em out here."

And so it was done. We snagged the pensioner and heaved him onto another body in another freezer which, it seemed, was not functioning particularly well.

"Listen," he then suggested resolutely, "I think it'd be a good idea to put your father on the bottom shelf because you are going to be back tomorrow morning, whereas they're going to come and pick up the agronomist in the afternoon."

"Fine," I agreed.

Thus, we were forced to lug the agronomist around again, me grasping his head and Adonis his feet. But the head was frozen so firmly that the moment we had raised him above us to slide him onto the upper shelf, he slipped out of my hands and, as a result, out of Adonis's, too, despite the latter's skillful attempts to hold onto him. The body of the agronomist crashed to the cement floor, causing a terrible thudding din. He was now lying facedown, and one of his arms was out of joint.

"Sorry," I gasped ruefully.

"Why've you gone so pale?" he inquired calmly. "It's nothing serious. Don't worry about it. If you knew how many times this has happened to me! And you know why? It's because I really freeze them properly."

"What about the arm?" I ventured.

"Which arm do you mean? I'll get it back into place in a minute. No one'll know about the fracture." Adonis set to work. It was not an easy task. At one point, he had to stand with one foot on the fellow's chest in order to wrench the arm back into place. I could hear the agronomist's bones creaking and cracking as Adonis huffed and puffed.

"Can I help?" I asked.

"No, no, just stomp on it for a moment, will you, so that it doesn't slide away. It's no problem. Such things happen," he continued. "And do you know why?"

"Because they are frozen solid," I replied.

"Bravo, that's it," he affirmed, breathing heavily. "I think we're finished," he added.

To raise the agronomist this time, he seized the head himself.

I was shaken to see that the corpse's nose was misshapen. Adonis noticed my shock and asked impatiently: "What's wrong now?"

"Look at the nose," I stammered.

"So what's wrong with the nose? Maybe it was like that from the start. There are lots of people with crooked noses," he declared, "but I must admit I don't remember the agronomist's being quite that out of keel."

We finally hefted the agronomist carefully onto the right tray.

I felt completely empty.

I went over to my father's body. Out of the corner of my eye, I saw Adonis fiddling with the agronomist's face. As soon as he noticed that I was watching him, he smiled reassuringly at the corpse as if to say "Everything will be all right now," and then leaned towards me, saying, "I think we're done."

I had the vague impression that in his mind he was straightening out my nose, too.

After much struggle, we hoisted my father onto the second shelf of the special freezer. As the door was closing, I had a final look at his face. I was leaving him all alone in that cold, dark chamber, in the company of persons unknown.

While I was pondering on the eternity of our separation, Adonis, holding the door ajar, gave me an inquiring look and asked an unusual question.

"Who did your father?"

"Who what? I don't understand the question."

"Your father, who did him?" he repeated, trying to make himself clear.

I was confused, and replied, "My grandmother. She gave birth to him."

"I don't mean who gave birth to him. I mean, who made up the body?"

I finally grasped what he was getting at and recalled how young girls were made up with cosmetics as brides when they got married.

"Oh," I replied tentatively, "probably the women. . . . I don't know."

He stared at me gloomily for a moment and added in a brusque tone, "Because they didn't do a very good job. In fact, I don't think he's even been made up. Of course, it's your decision. I'm not forcing you. It's your father after all, but to show him proper respect and not to do him up . . . but it's your choice. . . ."

I now realized what he was driving at and handed him another five thousand leks.

"It would be kind of you if you could do it."

"As you wish," he said, pacified. "You go and get yourself a cup of coffee and I'll finish the job. Come around afterward and give me a drive home, will you?"

I returned an hour later. He had finished with my father and had put him back into the freezer.

Adonis lived on the outskirts of town in an apartment on the second floor of a grimy, dust-covered tenement building. He insisted that I drive him right up to the entrance, and he did not get out right away. Having made certain that the whole neighborhood had noticed his arrival, he emerged from the car with great commotion and shouted, "Come around and pick me up tomorrow at seven. Right here!" Then he lumbered up the stairs under the respectful and no doubt jealous eyes of the neighbors.

I drove back home utterly exhausted and did not sleep well either. Every time I woke up, I thought about my father lying in that freezer, slowly turning to ice.

The next morning I went to pick up Adonis. I had to honk several times before he appeared at the window in his underwear. After surveying the entire street, he hollered, "Oh, you're already here! I'll be down in five minutes, as soon as I've finished breakfast."

He slumped into the car with a "How are you doing?" and spoke not a word all the way to the morgue. When we arrived, Adonis glanced around the yard, and I had the impression that he was on the lookout for bodies.

Of a passerby he inquired, "Have you come to see me?"

"You? Who are you?" asked the man.

"I work here at the morgue," replied Adonis.

"No. I have nothing to do with you. I am here to repair the walls."

"Oh, sorry," retorted Adonis, turning to me. "Let's go and get your father."

He yanked open the freezer door in a casual manner. My father was inside, completely frozen.

Adonis broke my silence, saying matter-of-factly, "Well, what do you think?"

"What can I say?" I asked, dazed.

"Go ahead, touch him."

I did so. The body was terribly cold. It had lost all its human warmth once and forever. Adonis waited for my reaction.

"It is very well frozen, I must say," I mumbled and requested that he help me carry the body out to the car. At that moment, however, another corpse arrived, so I had to ask the mason to assist me. I thanked Adonis once again as we were departing, with my father's coffin on our shoulders.

He gave me a cursory wave, as if to say, "Come around anytime!" and went on explaining the merits of his character to the relatives of the newly arrived deceased, stressing that he never took money without doing a proper job, and would never cheat anyone. As he spoke, Adonis led them over to the freezer which contained the body of the young girl, ready to confer the same demonstrative whack he had given her frozen face the previous day.

THE COUPLE

Ylljet Aliçka

WHENEVER AN OLD COUPLE FROM THE COUNTRYSIDE, DRESSED IN their finest clothes and smelling of mothballs, is invited to attend a wedding in the capital city, it is because the organizers of the wedding are obliged to do so for custom's sake. In this particular case, the old couple in question fully merited the invitation because they were the only surviving paternal relatives of the bride.

The wife was delighted at the invitation and said so openly, although it was not her direct relatives who were getting married. Her husband, the head of the household, reacted solemnly.

"Get my good clothes out, will you?" It was more than evident from his reply that he wanted to attend alone. His wife contradicted his plan immediately.

"If you are worried about the costs, I have enough money for the journey into town. And what would you do in the big city all by yourself anyway?"

"What concern is that of yours?" he retorted. "The wedding is going to take place in a restaurant and there will be no need for your help. In fact, it is not really customary . . ."

"What do you mean by 'not customary'?" she countered angrily. "They don't invite women there just to help in the kitchen, as they do in the countryside. In fact, it is not customary for a man to attend without his wife. In the city, they all go as couples. Didn't you know that?"

He was a taciturn and rather stoic individual.

"No, I didn't," he muttered, and asked for the key to the chest where they kept their money.

Knowing him well, she began sobbing and wiping her tears with a white kerchief conveniently at hand.

They had both been born in the same village and had gotten married there. Their only son had since departed and they had been living by themselves for some time. The couple were liked by the rest of the village. They were a hardworking pair and got along with one another, most of the time without saying a word. In fact, they rarely spoke—only the essentials.

The wife satisfied her female passion for gossip with the other women of the village, with whom she worked in a brigade.

The husband was wont to return home after work, light himself a cigarette, have a glass of wine with some cheese, and ponder on the order of things in this world.

"I am going to pass away and will never have been to the capital," she lamented. This charged statement caused him to stare at her for a moment. Then he said, "All right, come along, if you must." She jumped for joy and hastened to get her finest dress out of the closet.

At the village store they asked for the "best and most expensive present for a wedding in the city," which turned out to be a vase of artificial flowers that looked almost real. The present was duly enveloped in transparent wrapping paper with little blossoms on it, which rustled as they carefully carried it home.

With all the preparations and excitement, it was late before they got to sleep on the night preceding their departure.

The next day, a Saturday morning, they set off before dawn, having hardly slept a wink.

They journeyed into town on the back of a pickup truck. The wind had disheveled their hair and they were soon covered in a thin layer of dust. From time to time, they endeavored to shake it off, but the journey was long and the road was extremely dusty from start to finish. The old fellow stood in front of his wife, protecting her, his face turned to the wind, as if he were looking out at the distance. Every once in a while, he wiped the dust out of his eyes. She huddled against him, screened from the wind.

When they got into town, their faces were pale and their fine garments were filthy. The wrapping paper had been torn to shreds.

The first thing they did when they got off the truck was to clean themselves up. She took out a kerchief and spit into it to wipe off her husband's suit. This she did with swift and dexterous movements, as he stood there, looking away from her.

He had turned his eyes to the distant mountains.

"Aren't you finished yet? That's enough, woman," he muttered.

"Wait a moment. No one is watching, and we've got the whole day on our hands," she replied, continuing her work with devotion. "Just look at your shoes. Go and get them brushed off at the shoe shiner's over there." He agreed and sat down at the stall of a nearby shoe shiner, while she wiped her face in the window of a kiosk.

The couple arrived at the bride's home four hours early, and were received courteously. Rather embarrassed, he plunked the vase with the shredded wrapping paper onto the table and took his place ceremoniously in the armchair assigned to him.

"Oh, you shouldn't have bought a present," stammered the bride's father in routine fashion.

The couple murmured an appropriate response, not without pride in their voices.

A young girl then entered the room. She picked up the present with due care, in order not to soil her clothes, and held it in her outstretched fingers where the wrapping paper was not too shredded and dusty, pacing toward the other end of the parlor, where she placed it on a cupboard. The rustling of the paper could be heard all the way into the other room.

"So when did you get into town?" someone asked.

"Just today," they replied in unison. After a further half hour of silence, the old lady gave her husband an awkward glance and turned to the other women:

"Is there anything I can do to give you a hand?"

"No, nothing at all," replied a young girl. "The banquet is going to be held at a restaurant." There was silence once again in their corner of the room. Other guests arrived and were made welcome. Two hours before dinner, the couple decided to stretch their legs and go out for a walk.

They arrived at the restaurant one hour before the appointed time and got in everyone's way.

Someone showed them to two seats in a corner. Thereafter, everyone forgot about them.

The old lady tried to spark a conversation with her neighbor, a rather portly woman. The latter was, however, more interested in joking around and dancing than in conversing with two old people from the countryside.

He ate a little and drank a bit of raki, retaining an air of distinction. From time to time, he listened to the imprecations of a good-looking and elegantly dressed young man who, in choice vocabulary, was expounding on the necessity of psychological and social analysis to reach an understanding of the phenomenon of crime in Albanian society.

As he expounded on his theory, the young man dexterously waved his impeccably white hands and pink nails, which made it more than apparent that he spent much of his time caring for his outward appearance.

The young man with the fine hands continued, "It is senseless to try to condemn and castigate social evils nowadays. I think, and I am quite convinced of this, that crime in our society derives from the lack of a social contract. Only this would provide us with a definitive solution to the ills of our society and nation."

The people listened to his ideas respectfully and nodded. A young girl sitting a short distance away stared at the handsome gentleman with sorrow in her eyes. It was unclear whether the sorrow derived from the said ills of our society and nation or was the result of some fleeting emotion she felt as she listened to his impassioned words.

After a while, the old man lost interest. There was no more hint of feeling to be seen in his face.

The old couple said nothing throughout most of the dinner.

They ate as much as they could, and, when they had had their fill, the old woman took out a plastic bag to stuff it with leftover meat.

"What do you think you are doing?" he admonished angrily. "What are you doing? You are going to put us to shame in front of all the people. We are here in the city."

"I thought we could take a little something with us for lunch tomorrow. Look, everyone is doing it," she pleaded. It must be said that all the other guests, even those from the city, were indeed filling their bags with food and drink.

"You see," she said as the other guests were leaving, "we are the only ones who got nothing."

"They can take whatever they want, but we are not taking any-thing," he interrupted. They stayed until the early hours of the morning because they did not want to spend money on a hotel room. At dawn, they finally departed at the same time as the rock-and-roll group.

The bus back to the village was due to leave at four in the after-noon. For fear of thieves, they went into a café on the outskirts of town. There, they had coffee and sat around to pass the time.

At eight o'clock, they got up and left or, more precisely, were en-couraged to leave. The waiter pretended to have to sweep the floors around their feet and in doing so, raised an inordinate amount of dust with his broom.

The old lady was about to protest to the barman, but her husband rose to his feet.

"Don't bother," he said. "It is probably custom here."

"What sort of custom is that? They are just trying to get rid of us because we are from the countryside. I am going to give him a piece of my mind and, on top of that, he did not hand us our change. There are ten leks missing. You can see it in his face, he's a heartless thief." They set off, not knowing quite where to go.

The old couple meandered through the streets, looking at store windows until the afternoon. When the heat was at its zenith, they resolved to take a city bus to the overland bus station.

They waited and waited. The city bus was late and the heat had become unbearable.

"Come along, we'll walk it," he rasped, setting off.

"Where? It's too far!" she protested and followed behind him, tak-ing little steps. In no time, they were drenched in perspiration. He wiped his brow with a folded handkerchief and continued down the road in a noble manner. She panted and shouted at him, having dif-ficulty making herself understood.

"Slow down. Do you want to kill me? I'm exhausted." He contin-ued in large paces.

"Hold on for a moment, will you? You're not listening. Stop!" she shouted.

"What's wrong?" he eventually asked.

"What do you mean, what is wrong? Can't you see I am exhausted. You are acting as if someone is chasing us. We still have three hours until the bus leaves."

He slowed down and stopped at a crossroads, not knowing which direction to take. Gasping, she eventually caught up with him and uttered, "It must be that way, to the left."

He set off to the right with his mouth wide open because of the dryness of the air. She plodded on, several paces behind him.

"Hold on, I can't go any further," she protested. "If I at least had a glass of water. There is not even a public fountain here. Get me a bottle of water, will you, or I am going to collapse here on the spot. Go, leave me. I am not taking another step!" The old fellow stopped at a store and bought his wife a bottle of water, handing it to her without saying a word. She gulped it down as he waited, looking into the distance.

She left the bottle half full for him. He took one sip. "Have it all, I don't want any more," she insisted, but he refused. She put the cap on the bottle and stuffed it into her purse.

Once again, the couple set off slowly. The heat was oppressive. They had not even got halfway down the road when she began complaining. The old fellow refused to listen this time and continued his march.

She gave him an ultimatum.

"I am not going another step. You go wherever you want. I can't walk anymore. Do you understand? I cannot go any further. Are you listening? I think I am going to faint." She would not give in, and went and sat down on the curb near an iron fence.

He continued walking, but then looked back. Seeing that she would not budge, he returned to her.

The old fellow stood there for a while and looked around hesitantly before sitting down on the curb himself, two or three meters away from her.

She approached him. He said nothing and continued staring into the distance.

There were few people out on the road. The rare pedestrian passed by indifferently.

The old woman initially leaned against his shoulder, seemingly exhausted.

He murmured something or other.

"What?" she asked in a daze.

"Nothing," he replied. She snoozed. He murmured something once more.

"What did you say?" she inquired again.

"What are you doing, woman? Can't you see that people are staring? You should be ashamed of yourself," he blustered.

"Ashamed of what? What am I doing? I'm exhausted. We didn't sleep a wink all night." Saying this, she did something that shocked her husband deeply. She rested her head on his knee.

He blushed and griped, "What are you doing, woman?"

The old lady had fallen asleep and was breathing deeply. He gave her a glance and then continued staring into the distance. He took another look at her and pondered on the order of things in this world.

She snored lightly and snuggled against him. Her head was about to fall off his knee.

Embarrassed, the old fellow then did something he had never done before. He showed affection to a woman in public. Placing his rough hand on her head, he stroked her gray hair ever so gently. She seemed to sense the gesture and gave a sigh of satisfaction. She was now sound asleep.

The sun shone mercilessly, melting the pavement in front of them.

■ □ ■ □ ■

FERIT THE COW

Fatos Lubonja

I

Not many in the camp knew Ferit's real surname. We called him "the Cow." To hear his real name used by one of the guards was always a surprise, and this Ferit Avdullai seemed a different person from Ferit the Cow. He was big-boned and fat, with a strange long-headed skull, protruding eyes, and a broad jawbone. He even ate like a cow. At first sight, you would think this was the reason for his nickname, but in fact he was called "the Cow" because of one of those stories, half-dream and half-reality, that Ferit kept inventing, and which passed through the camp by word of mouth.

Ferit was from the picturesque lakeside village of Lin near Pogradec. He had been the village thief. In this sort of place, you might imagine people fishing, tending vineyards, or rowing boats, but not thieving. However, there was an agricultural cooperative, and there were cooperative thieves. Ferit's nickname dated back to the theft of a cow from the cooperative. He told how the cow had to pass through some mud, and they stuffed its hooves in two pairs of boots pointing backwards, to make false tracks. The next day, the whole village was astonished to find the cow gone. That was Ferit's story. Later, he added something. The cow had refused to move, and they had put green spectacles on its nose to make the mud in front of it look like grass. That is why we called him "the Cow," but this nickname would never have stuck were it not for the great hanging paunch that gave his belly such a bovine appearance.

Ferit had come to the prison camp at Spaç from a camp for common criminals, where he had served several short sentences for theft. Then they had accused him of agitation and propaganda against the regime. He had started life in the ordinary prisons when he was very young. He was now over fifty, and still had about twenty years left to serve. This was because, after he came to Spaç, they sentenced him to a second term for taking part in the revolt of 1973. Witnesses to the rebellion said that Ferit's only part in it was to try to loot the camp shop.

Even in the political prison, he did not give up his old trade. He pilfered whatever he could. Few of his fellow prisoners resented his thefts and hardly anybody thought of denouncing him to the camp guards. His petty thefts were generally tolerated, because of his crazy stories. Yet it was one of these fictions, the one about the chess pieces, that led him into trouble, and thereafter his life took a turn for the worse.

2

Nobody had ever heard Ferit talk about a wife or children, his mother or father, or brothers and sisters. This made him the kind of prisoner whom you could not imagine with any kind of life outside prison. Whenever he talked about women, Ferit mentioned Sanije and Xhevrije, the two loves of his life. In fact, they were two well-known whores in the camps for common criminals. He never went into details of sex, but would boast of how Sanije and Xhevrije were so canny and shrewd in everyday life. He would start telling you stories about them by calling you "our mate," "Now Sanije, our mate, . . . " or "Xhevrije, our mate, . . . " As time passed, Ferit started addressing almost every prisoner with the expression "our mate," and others began using it to him. "How are things, our mate?" "All right, our mate." The expression, implying membership of the same pack of ruffians, seemed to aid communication on both sides. But there was in fact a great gulf between Ferit and his fellow prisoners. "Our mate" was a rare beast, who lived in the camp entirely according to his own laws; he used this expression more as a mask for his activities, because he knew that he was nobody's mate. He was never seen to share a bit of bread at the same table with anyone. Most prisoners spoke to him only either to trigger a joke or out of fear that he would steal from them. But nobody was safe from his pilfering; Ferit was totally unable to resist the temptation to pinch anything that caught his eye.

Ferit most often plied his trade in the washroom. It had three sections: dishes and clothes were washed in the middle, and the lavatory cubicles and showers were on either side. The washroom was one of the busiest places in the camp, because all three shifts came here at different times to wash their dishes. There was an incessant coming and going to the latrine or to wash clothes and people waiting in line for showers. The water fell in trickles through holes drilled in pipes, which were positioned above a sort of broad gutter raised on bricks and cement. Above the pipes was a set of metal shelves, on which the prisoners placed their dishes or clothes while waiting their turn to wash them in the wooden tubs. It was the shelves that attracted Ferit to this place. He looked out for the flasks or plastic mugs the prisoners left there. These flasks and mugs were very valuable camp items because they were not provided by the authorities, who issued only one aluminum bowl and a spoon. Families had to bring them. They were extremely handy: the flask held drinking water or oil, and all sorts of things went into the plastic mugs. Ferit would hover about the washroom for hours on the lookout for somebody who might forget about his things while absorbed in conversation, or in the lavatory. Then he would snatch his loot, stuff it in his bag, and vanish. The prisoner might notice immediately, or only the next day when he needed his flask again. He would remember leaving it on the iron shelf. If he did not find it there, his first thought would be to ask Ferit.

"Ever seen a flask round here, our mate?"

"No, our mate."

"There's a mugful of sugar for you if you find it, our mate."

"Let's have a look, our mate. I saw a flask, but I don't know if it's yours."

Of course you had to hand over a portion of sugar or oil for Ferit to produce the utensil.

3

Ferit often ended up in the cooler. This was mostly on account of Pjetër Koka, the only camp guard who called him by his real surname, Avdullai. Pjetër was the most cunning of all in tracking down breaches of the regulations, and Ferit was one of his favorite quarries. He would stop him regularly and take him to one side for a detailed search. Ferit wore a camp-issue jacket with layers of patches stitched one over another. These patches also served as pockets, so he had two or three times as many pockets as anyone with the usual camp jacket. He would hide stolen oddments in these patched pockets, which were always filthy. In spite of the disgusting, grimy jacket, Pjetër Koka made no bones over stopping Ferit and searching him. First he would thrust his hands into the countless pockets, and then order him to open his bag. It was unusual for Ferit to get away without some contraband being found on him. He had all sorts of things in his patched pockets. Besides cigarette papers, which he traded freely, you might find razor blades, little pieces of mirror, nails, and stones. A sliver of razor blade or a fragment of mirror was enough to send him to the cooler for a month.

Ferit's trade in mirrors was one of his most successful enterprises. Nobody knew where he found them, but he always had a few in his bag. Some said that he stole them from the guards' pockets and broke them. He could sell a splinter for several packets of tobacco. The ban on mirrors in the camp was inexplicable, because there was no shortage of ordinary glass. The most likely reason was that it was one of the authorities' attempts to reduce all forms of pleasure to a minimum, like the ban on wearing civilian clothes. The prisoners could not resist the desire to see themselves, even in a tiny fragment that showed only a part of your face. Ferit too had his own mirror, a little larger than the ones he sold, and you could often find him studying the deep furrows in his brow and the fatty bags under his eyes. Pjetër Koka played with Ferit like a cat with a mouse, and might let him off for a nail in his bag or pocket, but whenever he found him with a tiny mirror he sent him straight to the punishment cell.

Sometimes Pjetër searched Ferit even in the cooler itself. Ferit always submitted abjectly to Pjetër's hunting zeal. It was perhaps this very subservience that excited Pjetër's sadism as he searched him with a wry smile, certain of finding some illegal trophy. Pjetër never imagined that Ferit might resist him, and still less that this ragged figure might take his revenge one day through a fantastical story, and his sadistic gratification would turn to fury.

Ferit's fantasies most often came to him in the punishment cell. Of course, there was an explanation for this. The camp had four cells, each about two meters long and one and a half meters wide. The inmate had to sit there the whole day, without any respite apart from the three meals, each followed by a trip to the lavatory and the issue of a cigarette. He was deprived of newspapers, books, the radio, electric light, and all extra food. He was given only one ladle of broth in the morning and at midday, and one ladle of sugarless tea in the evening, with a hunk of bread. The only light in that concrete box came from the small peephole in the door, and after dusk this was not enough to distinguish the face of a person opposite you. Pjetër Koka called the cells "nests." He would threaten prisoners by saying, "Do you miss the nest?" In summer, he would shove four or five men into each of these nests, where they sweltered in the stifling heat. In winter, he would put in only one or at the most two, to prevent them from warming each other with their breath and body heat. Many prisoners preferred a humiliating beating or several hours in handcuffs screwed tight to the bone to time in the cells. After one month in the cell, you needed two months to recover your strength.

These nests probably encouraged Ferit's rampant imagination, because he had so much less chance to steal or eat. Once he came out of the cell with a dream that prisoners told to each other for a long time afterward. In his dream, Ferit had seen the craggy hills of the mine turned into mountains of pilaf. In the middle, there was a lake of yogurt, and Ferit had eaten and drunk from these hills with a spoon made of a mine wagon. It was not clear whether this was a dream, or something that Ferit had made up, but for a long time it transformed the landscape of Spaç in the prisoners' eyes.

Ferit devised a lot of these fantasies. He did not circulate them himself. He merely announced them when they came to him, and then somebody would pick them up and pass them around the camp. He would only retell them when asked, and then only after persistent encouragement. However, just like his expression "our mate," these dreams too were a mask. Nobody could discover what really went on in this man's mind. Most of Ferit's fellow prisoners found entertainment in his stories, but our mate remained an outsider, entirely isolated. He never talked to anybody for more than a few moments at a time, and then mostly to prisoners wanting to hear his fantasies yet again, or to trade a mirror, cigarette papers, or a stolen plastic mug. Nor did our mate show any desire to spend more time with anybody. When he started his stories, he would brighten a little, but he knew his place and would often slope off once he had mentioned Sanije or Xhevrije, who had once made him the apple of their eye. His only significant contact with other people was through his fantasies, and it was these that determined his fate, for good or ill.

5

The story of the chess pieces, Ferit's most famous and successful tale, was in fact not an embroidered fantasy. It derived from an incident in a cell, and a quick retort that showed that this man's brain was not entirely concentrated on the search for food. It brought Ferit closer to his fellow prisoners than at any time before, but its great success also had fatal repercussions.

During one of his frequent punishments, as always after being searched by Pjetër, Ferit was put in a cell with two other prisoners, who played chess all day. Every cell inevitably had a chessboard, scratched into the floor by a sharpened spoon handle or other sharp object that had been smuggled in. The pieces would be squeezed out of the crumb of the bread, some mixed with cigarette ash to tell black from white.

Ferit had been left for several days with the two chess players, who paid no attention to him. There was nothing there to steal or to eat, so Ferit had gobbled up the dry chess pieces. The players were dozing at the time. They woke up and hunted for their pieces. Failing to find them, they looked at Ferit, who said that he had eaten them.

"Why did you eat them, our mate?"

"I was hungry, our mate. When the ration comes, I'll give you some of my bread so you can make new ones."

They knew that when Ferit's crust came, he would devour it in an instant.

A moment later, one of the chess players noticed that there were two uneaten pieces, still left on the floor.

"But why didn't you eat these two, our mate?"

Ferit opened his eyes wide. Of course, he had missed them. He picked them up. One was a pawn and the other a bishop.

"I didn't eat these," he said, "because this little one looked like that nice Lazër, and this bishop looked like Ali."

Lazër was the most decent of the camp guards, while Ali was the camp bookkeeper, who was always very courteous and spoke little to the prisoners.

The incident became famous in the camp. "But which one did you eat first?" the prisoners asked when Ferit came out. "Pjetër Koka," Ferit replied.

After this story, Ferit was forgiven all the harm he had done, pinching rubber mugs, flasks, and other odds and ends. But he paid a heavy price for this last joke at Pjetër Koka's expense. The rumor that Ferit had eaten all the officers and guards, except for Ali and little Lazër, reached the ears of the authorities. One of Pjetër Koka's many spies passed it on to him, and the latter reacted with his nasty smile, "I will send Ferit Avdullai down to a place where he won't have a chance to eat or steal." He meant Burrel Prison. The opportunity came soon.

Our mate was not aggressive or violent. When you caught him with your mug, he would say at once that he had not known it belonged to "our mate" and give it to you without a murmur. So the whole camp was surprised one day when he pulled a stone out of his bag and hit Fetah on the head. It was a few days before Fetah was due to be released. He ended up in the sick bay, and soon left, and so told nobody why Ferit had hit him. Ferit spent another month in the cells, but said nothing about why he had struck out in this way. The story went that, many years previously, Fetah had beaten him up, and Ferit had waited to take revenge until just before his release, so that Fetah would have no time to pay him back. We all knew that our mate had the courage of a chicken, but nobody believed that he could harbor a grudge for so long. In fact, nobody knew what was on Ferit's mind that day. Some said that Fetah, with a raging thirst, had hogged the tap for half an hour and left Ferit to wait so long that he lost his temper. But we could not believe this either. The secret behind this blow lay hidden in Ferit's impenetrable depths.

Normally, an act of this kind meant a month in the punishment cell. As soon as Ferit came out of the cooler, they took him away to Burrel Prison. Everybody was surprised, but then remembered Pjetër Koka's vow. The blow to Fetah's head became Pjetër's pretext to strike in revenge for the story of the chess pieces. This tale was still successfully going the rounds not only in Spaç but beyond, as transferred prisoners carried it to other camps and prisons.

6

Ferit received a warm welcome from the prisoners of Burrel, because his fantastical stories had gone before him from Spaç. He was also able to get his teeth into some food from family parcels, because the custom in Burrel was that anybody who had a visit would treat each of his roommates. But there were not many visitors to Burrel, and there were no more than ten prisoners to a room, most of them bored and hungry. In fact, Burrel was a terrible prison for anybody without parcels. Ferit very soon understood what he had brought on himself by eating Pjetër Koka in the form of a chess piece. Above all, he had to find tobacco; he had kept himself supplied in the camp by trading in mirrors and other odds and ends. He started to sell his bread ration to buy handfuls of tobacco, and for food he relied on leftovers given to him by prisoners who received visits or large parcels. When he was short, he would collect the stubs of cigarettes. He would cut them open, dry the contents, and smoke them rolled in newspaper.

As time passed, his hunger became more ravenous, but he could not easily steal. He was under his fellow prisoners' gaze all day.

He began to waste away; his ribs showed, and his nickname "the Cow" fitted him better than ever. One of his ribs was indeed as thick as a cow's. Yet strangest of all was his physical immunity. When any of the food brought by their families spoiled, his roommates would testily throw it into the garbage pail in the corner. They would not dare give it to Ferit for fear of poisoning him, even though he begged for it persistently. Ferit himself would retrieve it from the pail and eat it. Amazingly, nothing happened to him.

The man was insatiable. His mind got to work on schemes to obtain food through his old, and only, trade of theft. But how to steal in a room where you were always in the company of your fellow prisoners?

So Ferit began to suffer a calvary of beatings at the hands of the other prisoners. The first to beat him up was a prisoner with no parcels. While waiting to fetch his soup from the canteen, he had left his bowl near the door, and was finishing a game of chess. There were two spoonfuls of oil in the bowl, which another prisoner had given to him to thicken the prison broth. Meanwhile, Ferit paced back and forth from the wall to the door with his bread ration in his hand, and whenever he passed the bowl he would dip his bread in the oil and continue his pacing, munching the oil-smeared crust. After he had passed several times, somebody noticed this and shouted at him. The other prisoner found that the oil was gone. In the camp, this might be taken as a joke, but not in Burrel. The victim seized his bowl and struck Ferit on the head with it several times. Our mate did not react.

The beatings became more frequent. Prisoners with family visits, who had been generous to him in the past, were the angriest of all; Ferit would promise not to touch their food, and still they found themselves robbed. Ferit never struck back, but only protected himself. Normally, he got off lightly because the beatings were perfunctory. In no time the warden would come, open the peephole, and catch the assailants in the act.

When he found he could not hide any of his thefts, Ferit chose another method. He stayed awake at night and ate the food that the prisoners kept underneath their bedboards. When they had fallen asleep, Ferit would get up and rummage among all the bowls he could find. The prisoners raised the alarm when they woke in the morning. They knew that our mate had stolen from them. This was more a form of plunder than theft, and Ferit admitted that it was hunger that drove him to it.

One day the prisoners found that all their bowls had vanished. Ferit had emptied their contents and stuck them under a stair in the exercise yard. This time, several people jumped on him. Ferit bent his back, hid his head under his arms, and endured it all without making a sound. The prisoners vented all their fury. The warden did not interrupt, and must have been in the exercise yard. Then they hung back. They thought they had made mincemeat of him, but amazingly Ferit stood up and straightened his back. He started hunting all over the place, bending his head to the floor and muttering,

"Where did I drop that cigarette? Where did I drop that cigarette?" (It was the cigarette he had lit before they had jumped upon him.)

It was because he provoked fights of this kind that the authorities started moving Ferit from one room in the prison to another. His presence in any room turned life into a nightmare. In the camp, the prisoners had been able to keep their distance from him, but here the presence of this almost bestial creature at close quarters was exhausting. The least of it was that nobody could keep any sort of food in the room, to break the monotony of the day. Anyone in the same room as Ferit simply had to leave his food in the storehouse outside. Worse, in each of the rooms where Ferit went, some prisoner would end up in a punishment cell on his account, because sooner or later someone would beat him up and be caught by the warden. People became convinced that the governor was using Ferit to punish prisoners he disliked. Yet Ferit himself often ended up in the cells too.

It was when he came out of one of the cells in winter that he told his most famous fantasy of his time in Burrel. It was freezing cold in the cell. The icicles that hung from the prison roof penetrated the grille and hung down close to his head. His belly was racked by hunger. One night he saw himself in a dream, covered by a great quilt made of pastry. Hungrily, he started to eat the upper edge that covered his neck. But this made the crust smaller, and his feet stuck out from the bottom and froze. All night long, he wrestled with the pastry, eating it from the top and stretching it with his feet at the bottom. He had devoured it all when dawn came and he woke up frozen to the bone.

For a time, this fantastical dream eased his relations with his fellow prisoners. They cheerfully overlooked some of his nightly thefts. However, their earlier hostility soon returned. The prisoners of Burrel lived on their nerves. It was because of Ferit that two more prisoners were sent to the cells. One night, he ate the food of one of his roommates, a prisoner whom he had promised to leave alone. The next day, he had refused to take the blame and accused two other prisoners who slept opposite him. These two threw themselves onto him, punching and kicking. The warden opened the peephole at that very moment, caught them in the act, and one hour later took the men away and shoved them in a cell.

The entire room was furious. They would stomach no more. When the warden closed the door, leading his two most recent victims away to the cells, the inmates of the room devised a plan. They would beat Ferit to the verge of death. Ferit's final victim, who had lost all the meat brought by his family, got ready for action by putting on a pair of army boots. Ferit sat on his bed, guiltily hanging his head, unaware of the beating in store, the likes of which he had never known. The prisoners jumped on him, kicking and punching in a wild frenzy. He was thrown from his bunk to the ground. The warden opened the peephole, but still the prisoners did not stop. This time, they had decided they would all go to the cells. At times like this, the wardens did not interfere. Ferit lay on the floor, the prisoners kicking him all over his body, and in the head. But they knew from experience that he always bounced back. The prisoner in the army boots climbed onto the bunks and hurled himself with his full weight on Ferit's body, again and again, until he heard a crack. The prisoners fell back. Ferit lay still. Not a sound came from him. Never before had he failed to stand up after a beating. Now that the uproar was over, the warden opened the door and ordered the prisoners to put him outside.

The doctor diagnosed severe bruising, two broken ribs, and a serious fracture of the pelvis.

When Ferit came out of the hospital several months later, he was not sent back to Burrel, but to the camp. Strangely, he no longer stole and had lost his insatiable appetite. He made do with the camp rations and the occasional morsel he was given. Nor did he tell any fantastical stories. He was an ordinary prisoner who had suddenly discovered that he was an old man. If one of the long-term prisoners who had known him in the past asked him to tell how he had eaten the chess pieces, or the dream with the mountains of pilaf or the pastry quilt, he would sit and listen as if these stories had nothing to do with him. It was only when you mentioned Sanije and Xhevrije that he would smile a little and say, yes, they knew what life was and how to give a man a good time.

■ □ ■ □ ■

AN AMERICAN DREAM

Stefan Çapaliku

I

"I'm going to sell my car and move to America. There is nothing left for me here. There's no sense in it anymore. . . . My wife and daughter are living there and I am stuck with my parents back here. It doesn't make any sense. I've done enough for them. I know they are getting old, but they've also got my sister, not just me. Let her take care of them for a change. That's the only solution. After all, you only have one life. What do you think?"

These are the words I hear almost every morning from my neighbor, right after I leave my apartment building. He knows that I have my morning coffee at the café next door and is on the lookout for me every day. I am pretty sure that sooner or later I am going to have to change cafés. I haven't changed up to now because I believed what he said, that he would very soon sell his car, abandon his parents, and finally join his wife and daughter in America.

But every morning, his old car, that Fiat Uno, remains parked out front. In the café sits Cufi with his mustache, and over my balcony hangs the washing of his devoted mother.

I enter the café for my morning coffee, never in my life having drunk it at home, and Cufi pulls back a chair for me to sit on. The place is usually full of people I know. Cufi normally gets there at least an hour beforehand and waits for me, all his brilliant conversation being ignored by the people at the surrounding tables. He gives me a hearty welcome, in particular since I'm usually the one who pays for *his* morning coffee.

"Yes, Cufi . . . you're right . . . sell your car . . . leave your parents at your sister's place and get away. . . . Your wife and daughter are waiting for you." This, as you can imagine, is my daily spiel before I bid him farewell and set off for work.

2

I didn't know Cufi's wife. I had never even seen her . . . until he showed me her photograph one fine morning during the couple of minutes we spent at the café. I was thunderstruck, but I collected myself immediately. I pretended to be indifferent and to be staring at the waiter who was coming over with the bill.

"How can I get this photo enlarged? Where do they do that?" Cufi asked me right off.

"No problem," I replied. "I can scan it at my office. What format do you want it in?"

Cufi replied simply, "Make it as big as you can," and handed me the photo. I took it, seemingly indifferent, and put it in the inside pocket of my jacket.

"What's your wife's name, Cufi?"

"Anna," he replied, enunciating the two *a*'s differently from one another.

"Anna? All right. I'll try to get it done as soon as possible," I replied as I turned to leave.

God, she was the most beautiful woman I had ever laid eyes on! As soon as I could, I took the photo carefully out of my jacket and stared at it, without paying attention to where I was going. She was stunning. It was a silhouette portrait. She had her blonde hair tied up, and her lush lips were pressed against one another ever so gently. She had high cheekbones and large green eyes. Cufi's wife was the ideal woman. She was the being every man longed for in moments of fantasy.

"I'm going to sell my car and move to America. There is nothing left for me here. It doesn't make any sense. . . . What do you think?" I recalled Cufi's words. Who is this guy who hangs on here and doesn't try to get back to her as quickly as possible?

When I got to the office later, holding her photo in my hand, it occurred to me to buy his car, finance a home for his parents, and tell him, "Go ahead! What are you waiting for? After all, you only have one life. Get going!" It was with these thoughts that I began work. . . .

3

"You always luck out," said my boss as we stood at the top of the staircase. "I just get more and more bills and taxes to pay. You'll have to go to America in my place. Washington. Get the ticket yourself and go, tomorrow if you can. I have to be here to receive a high-level delegation. Damn it!" he continued, before entering his office.

Washington! I had just seen the word written on the back of the photo of Cufi's wife, Anna. Washington! And I was supposed to travel the very next day. I had no time left, not a minute. All I could do was put the photo back into my jacket and head home.

I didn't even have time to tell Cufi what had happened. I phoned my wife and began groping around in the upper shelves of the clothes closet for a suitcase. I also had to get my ticket and make the usual arrangements. My wife was not particularly fond of my sudden business trips, but she knew better than anyone else what a traveling husband needed.

4

When I got to the little airport, I discovered that I still had Anna's photo with me. It was in the inside pocket of my jacket where I usually keep my plane ticket and passport. They were all traveling together—the photo in my passport, her photo, and the ticket that was the means of shortening the distance between us.

It was not the first time that I had crossed the Atlantic. I knew what a torture it was, realizing full well that I was not one of those fortunate individuals who could sleep all the way, not even one of those who could immerse himself in a book for the length of the journey. On the contrary, I sat there, drowsy and confused, and entered a reality of my own creation, one which alternately elated and depressed me, but from which I inevitably emerged with a backache.

My confusion during this flight had almost reached the surreal. It was assisted no doubt by the fine weather, not a cloud in the sky, and by the strangely transparent atmosphere. From the time we left the continent, I stared out of the window at the shimmer of light moving along the surface of the ocean. And to follow that shimmer from an altitude of ten thousand meters means that it was really moving quickly. Then I closed my eyes and . . . later . . . in a light slumber, I began to imagine that the shimmer of light on the ocean below me was Cufi's car. Cufi had set off for America in his Fiat and, at the speed he was traveling, was likely to arrive before me. Even though he was in a Fiat, he was dressed like a pirate from the Middle Ages. He had lost one eye in the vanguard of a battle. The empty socket was covered by a black leather patch which was tied around the back of his head by a strap. He had a sash at his waist and was suitably armed: a dagger, a steel hook for boarding vessels, the type of hook which had gouged out his missing eye, and a pair of pincers to cut the throat of any sea captain who got in his way. I was not sure whether or not Cufi still had both arms. He was, at any rate, haughtier than I had ever seen him and had obviously changed his mind at the last minute and decided not to sell his car.

Later on, there was a moment when he looked up and recognized me. We gave one another an unusually friendly smile and waved, both acutely aware of what we were up to. . . .

5

The important meeting which had brought me so urgently to America lasted only two days, but they were so crammed with activity that I hardly had time to come up for breath. I only had one free day and would have to fly back home on the next. As I had nothing particularly important to say at the meeting, I remember spending my time thinking about where I would go on the third day. I got back to the hotel, exhausted after a dinner offered by the organizers. It must have been after midnight, though it was early morning by European time. Although I was desperately tired, I couldn't get to sleep at all. Alone, with my clothes scattered from one end of the room to the other, I remembered the photo. It was there on the dressing table. I took it and had another look. On the back side, there was something written: a name, an address, and a telephone number. Everything was at my disposal: a telephone, her number, I myself, she herself, the desire taking hold of me, and the photo. It was simply the time of day, or rather of night, which was out of line. "You have time on your hands tomorrow, don't you?" I asked myself. I did, but she might be at work and . . . and that would mean it would all be in vain. I did not even really understand my motive for needing to contact Cufi's wife.

"Hello? Anna . . . ? I'm sorry to bother you. I realize it's late, but . . . I'm . . . I just got here from Tirana and am only staying for a short time, actually just till tomorrow. And I thought you might have something you wanted me to take back for Cufi, or . . . if there's anything else I could do for you."

"How kind of you! Thanks very much. It would be a pleasure to meet you. It's been such a long time and I've been getting homesick . . . for Tirana and everything. Tomorrow? Tell me where you want us to meet and at what time. . . ." I heard her gentle, longing voice at the other end of the line.

I told her it would be convenient for us to meet at nine o'clock at the entrance to the Philips Collection, which was near my hotel.

"How will I recognize you?" she inquired.

"Oh, don't worry. I have a photo of you. I will recognize you right away."

6

I left the hotel at ten to nine, having spent almost the whole night wide awake, yet I felt a sense of release. I had nothing to take with me, no briefcase, nothing, and strolled down the road with my hands in my pockets. I was leaning against one of the columns at the entrance and would have felt like a local had not a tall, thin man passed by and greeted me in Russian with a "*zdrastvuyte.*" I smiled and answered him in Albanian. It then occurred to me that I had chosen the worst possible moment for our meeting because everyone was on his way to work. Masses of people were entering the building. This caused me to take the photo of Cufi's wife out of my pocket once more and have another glance at it. I watched the flow of people shuffling along. She was not going to keep the appointment, and I had the impression of being in one of those romances where you wait and wait in vain.

It was twenty past nine and there were still lots of people passing by, but she was not among them. She had not shown up. I took another look at the photo to assure myself that none of the pedestrians resembled her. It was at nine thirty that I caught sight of a small, thinnish woman in her forties. She looked weary as she approached and asked, "Hello, are you Albanian?" and then pronounced my name.

"I am Cufi's wife, Anna," she said.

Cufi's wife! Anna! She did not look like the woman in the photo at all. She was a completely different person.

I was dazed. I felt a numbness in my limbs and a dryness in my mouth. I don't know what impression I made on her, but I imagine I must have looked like someone who had just been jolted out of a deep sleep.

"How are you?" she asked, as she shook my hand.

"You didn't recognize me at all," she added. "I have been standing here for over half an hour." She smiled.

"Is that right? Me, too."

She seemed to sense the confusion and numbness within me.

"I wanted to tell you last night, but I forgot. I wanted to tell you that you could not possibly recognize me from a photo. I have changed a lot. . . ."

"No, you haven't," I muttered.

"Yes, I have. It's true. . . . Young girls, girls are like the breeze . . . ," she replied with a rueful look.

I was still bewildered as we strolled along the pavement. She was the only one to speak. I had forgotten everything I had wanted to say, both the compliments and Cufi's plans to sell his car and get back to his family.

In the end, she seemed to have had enough of me, lifeless idiot that I was, and did the best thing she could have done at that moment. She turned and shook my hand.

"All the best. Sorry I took up your time. It would be better not to say anything to Cufi. . . . Have a good flight. . . ."

7

I returned home the next day, filled with a sense of anguish and incredulity about what had taken place. I even forgot to buy something for my wife and the children. Nothing. I was completely exhausted.

The plane arrived early in the morning and I was home by about seven. I greeted everyone, had a glass of milk as usual, and left the house to go to work.

Cufi was waiting for me at the café. He offered me a chair and I joined him.

"I haven't seen you around," he said.

"I've been late for work the last couple of days. I wasn't feeling too well. . . . That's why. What about you?"

"I'm fine. Nothing special. But I've decided to sell my car and move to America. There is nothing left for me here. It doesn't make any sense. . . . My wife and daughter are living there and I am stuck with my parents back here. There's no sense in it. I've done enough for them. I know they are getting old, but they've also got my sister, not just me. Let her take care of them for a change. That's the only solution. After all, you only have one life. What do you think?"

THE MUTE MAIDEN

Lindita Arapi

HE IS DEAD NOW, AND THEY HAVE ALL GONE AWAY. I AM ALONE. NOW that its specter has vanished, I have moved into Mother's room. It was there that I wrote the tale of the mute maiden and have resolved never to speak again.

In the beginning, I did not understand what that decision really meant. I was actually only amused by the thought that everyone else would have to work hard at trying to understand me—that they would be frustrated and saddened. I saw myself as a wall of impenetrable silence they would never be able to break though. Later, the situation became unbearable for me, too—so unbearable that I thought I would burst and disintegrate. Sometimes I had the impression that my head had been split in two and that my brains were oozing out without my feeling it at all. This sensation became so strong on occasion that I was convinced my head was finally empty . . . and I was relieved.

It was at that time that the words, which used to flow out of me so profusely, began to wither and dry up until there was no sound left in me at all. Perhaps as a result, I began to put my thoughts to paper. One needs time for this new form of communication, and I am happy that I now have all the time I need. Nothing that bothers and torments other people in their daily lives worries me. I watch the days go by out on the veranda and puzzle at the forms and contortions of eyes and hands. I am amazed that the passing bodies still move the way they once did.

I don't know how long it has been. Quite a few days must have passed because I have forgotten a lot of what happened. The memories come back to me in fragments, and I cannot link them to one another or put them sufficiently in order to make any sense out of them. Nonetheless, I will try to retrieve what remains in the recesses of my mind and set the splinters free. Perhaps they will come to life again.

Whenever Father entered the room, we girls would stand up and drop whatever we happened to have in our hands on the bed—knitting or an apple with the first bite taken out of it. I would always close my book and, because I was the smallest, approach him to help him take off his jacket.

"Hi, Daddy. How was your day?" my elder sisters would say with a mixture of smiles, dread, and shyness on their faces.

I never managed to open my mouth at the proper time when he was in the room. An incomprehensible murmur lodged somewhere in the back of my throat whenever I gave him a hand to prepare for his nap. It was all part of the family rituals that began every morning when the door creaked open and the huge shadow of my father appeared in the hallway. Those rituals were nothing more than a way of getting the stagnant waters of family love and devotion flowing again. As far back as I can remember, we always took the same posture. There were always the same tokens of respect, the same fear, and the same tardy reaction on my part when my sisters greeted him. My habit of not opening my mouth at all when Father got back from work dates perhaps from that time. I never managed to greet him properly. All that succeeded in squeaking through my teeth was a meek "How was your day?" I would approach quietly to hang up his jacket and then fetch some hot water to wash his feet.

Whenever I knelt in front of him and massaged his feet swollen from his exhausting work, I would think how strange his toes looked. I wondered if I would recognize them if they were somewhere else. And then I would hear his deep and gentle voice inquiring about me.

"How were your marks at school today?"

I was good at school and rarely got bad marks. If I did, I did not try to conceal them, as my sisters did, but rather showed them off to my father. It amused me to watch him get upset, and I would listen to his tirade patiently without letting it bother me at all.

I remember the secret pleasure I took whenever I succeeded in putting him in a bad mood—whenever I stopped being Daddy's little girl.

"Where are your brains, child? You're not concentrating in class. Look at the marks you're getting!" he would shout.

"I never had any brains, Daddy," I would say, teasing him.

He would look nervous whenever the children he had raised, like his own flesh and blood as he was wont to say, began to use his words.

Every time I replied using his expressions, I was severely punished. I would be locked in the bathroom with nothing to eat until my father decided I had suffered enough. Sometimes the little pleasures I took with him were so severely punished that I spent the whole night in the bathroom, without light and heat. The bathroom was a terrifying place. Cowering in a corner in the dark, I would whine, afraid all the time that the neighbors would hear me. Abandoned in my little corner of the world, I remember praying fervently to a star I could see through the window, hoping that God would be there and heed my plight. I later took revenge by not talking to my father at all for days on end. My silence lasted even longer when I came to realize that he fully understood what fear and trepidation I suffered in the bathroom and continued to hold me captive there. My rebellion as a child went so far that I dreamed of running away, of forcing my desperate parents to search for me and comprehend at long last just how much they had hurt their little girl. My daydreams always ended like fairy tales. I would return home to my smiling and caring father, who would stroke my hair, and we would all live happily ever after.

I often recall the words of my mother. She held the view that I had long been my father's pet. Whenever he got back from work, he would always bring me a piece of chocolate or cake. Later, when he noticed that I was showing signs of maturity, he would talk to me as he would to a guest in his house—to someone he had to take care of.

After the death of my mother, my elder sisters got used to him and his melancholic silence. They accepted him the way he was and laughed at my worries when he changed his behavior toward me. They tended to his every need like two guardian angels for whom the word of a man was absolute.

I had only gotten used to his eternal silence, and whenever he did utter a word, I would take fright and drop what I had in my hands. I was amazed at how artificial he sounded when he spoke. I felt all right when he wandered about the house in silence, but I only really felt safe when he was in his own room. Then I was free to do whatever I wanted, to try on a new dress or to use my mother's lipstick.

The dark blue door to his room was usually kept locked, even when he was not at home. I had such a longing to sleep in that room again, as I had when Mother was alive, when she would let me snuggle up to her breast.

When I was forbidden to enter the room, it turned into a magic place. I would glance stealthily at the door whenever it opened, and I would look inside whenever my sisters entered to take my father his tea in the evening. At the time, I puzzled over why one sister would go in one evening and the other sister the next evening to take Father his dinner or to help him get ready for bed. Later I got used to the idea. It became a daily ritual, something which was simply done, in particular now that Mother was no longer alive. After all, someone had to look after my father. My sisters were grown up now, ready to take husband, as my aunt would say. They would spend their time knitting for their dowries and pondering about their future spouses. Their conversations were interrupted only when my father entered the room, at which time the subject immediately changed. It was unheard of in a house of girls to talk about men — that I knew — and for virgins, it was considered quite shameful.

"Father is the shame of the house," I would say, teasing them to drive them out of the room. But I was in fact the shameless virgin of the house, inspired by all the books I had read.

I viewed men at the time as suits of clothes cut out of colored paper. They were more intelligent than girls. That is why I drew them with two heads. I remember that when I showed the drawings to my sisters, they groaned and predicted I would have a hard time with men when I grew up.

"Meander from man to man she will. . . ."

"I'm going to have three husbands: one in a green suit, one in a blue suit, and one in a black suit like your girlfriend's husband." I would tell them all about my future husbands and make them laugh.

THE MUTE MAIDEN

"Look at her, she still has milk dripping from her lips," my eldest sister, Lily, would shout to tease me.

And that did infuriate me because I had been doing my utmost to appear older, especially with my friends, to whom I would reveal the love stories I had overheard from my sisters. "What do you mean by milk on my lips? All right, then I'm going to have one husband, just one husband," I stammered and ran out into the yard.

"Quiet. You'll be the shame of us all. Everyone is listening. Be quiet!"

But I paid no attention to them. The more they told me to keep quiet, the louder I would become.

"I want a husb . . . , husb . . . ," my voice trembled until I lost control of it completely and stammered, "house bird."

I looked up and suddenly saw my father staring at me. I lowered my head and waited for retribution to follow. But instead, he passed me by and went into the house, muttering, "Can't we find that girl a budgie or something? Otherwise she'll whine all day."

There I stood in the middle of the yard with a finger in my mouth, not at all relieved that I had not been punished. "Father had looked at me as if he had seen me for the very first time," I thought to myself for a moment, wondering at the strange father I had. Then I went off to the rabbit hutch to play with the animals I so loved. I could while away the hours there, talking to my tiny friends, as everyone called them. Whenever I was sad, I would go out to the rabbit hutch and tell them my problems.

I would have long forgotten this minor episode, had it not been the prologue of what was later to come.

I got up early that morning and was full of energy. No one else was at home, and I was glad that there would be nobody there to push me around. The fact that the day started out well was actually more related to events of the night before than to the fact that it was one of my rare mornings alone.

On the evening before, my aunt had given me some white lace panties, like the underwear the older girls wore. It was the first time that I had ever worn such clothes. I put them under my pillow and could hardly wait for my sisters to come home so that I could unfold them piously on the bed like a flag.

It was nine o'clock. I shuddered every time the metallic clang of the clock echoed through the house. Somehow, I hated the sound. It made me shiver, like a cold shower. I looked up automatically and saw a key turning in the door lock. It was my father.

He smiled when he saw me with some books in my hand. I acknowledged his presence curtly because I was waiting for my sisters to arrive. I wanted desperately to show my new secret to someone, and a novel, mysterious instinct made me speak.

I watched my father's steps as he went into the bedroom. He said nothing, obviously not wanting to make me nervous. I hesitated for a moment and then . . . walked toward the bedroom. Pushing the door ajar, I entered the room for the first time. He turned around, looking somewhat perplexed. "Hey, little girl, what are you trying to hide from me? Have you got a piece of candy or something?" he said jovially.

"No," I replied coyly and spread my new panties out for him to see. "Look what Auntie bought me. Look how nice they are. I'm going to wear them tomorrow for my birthday. Sonya wears them, and now I'm going to wear them, too." I beamed. "Like they wear when they get married," I added, posing with the panties in front of me.

I blabbered on and did not even notice the change in the expression on his face. It had flushed.

"Come on over here so that I can see you," he whispered.

"They're not like the clothes they show on TV," I said, approaching.

"This is the day you have been waiting for," he murmured, stroking the panties I was modeling. "You're on the lookout for a man. It won't be long now, I see. But before that . . . "

I stood back. "What are you doing, Daddy?"

Without warning, he threw me onto the bed with his hands of iron and began to rip off my clothes one by one. I cowered, petrified that he would choke me to death, and tried to push him away. "No, no, Daddy, no!"

"Listen, I was the one who gave you life. . . . I gave you your life, you know, and I am the first one to stroke you, to touch you and make you ready for a boyfriend." He could hardly breathe. "I want to be the first one. Then you can have the others, I. . . ." He foamed at the mouth and forced his way between my thighs.

THE MUTE MAIDEN

"No, you mustn't, Daddy!" I screamed, full of shame, despair, and disgust.

The ceiling began revolving like the globe in a geography class. The last things I saw were the oceans and continents spinning out of control.

When I opened my eyes, I was drenched in tears, all down my neck. There was a whisper in my ear. It was cold, so very cold. I got up slowly, pushing off his arms, which wanted to help me.

I did not know whether I still had a body or whether it had been blown away like the autumn leaves in the wind.

I turned to look at him once again. The distorted expression on his face struck me like a knife through the heart. He was so far away now.

"Father, I worshipped you. You gave me the gift of life and will always be first. But the day will come, Father, when you will pass away. And you will have to die soon, because if you don't, I will kill you with my bare hands. I will kill you, Father!"

Those were the last words I ever spoke.

■ □ ■ □ ■

THE SNAIL'S MARCH TOWARD
THE LIGHT OF THE SUN

Eqrem Basha

FROM HALF A METER AWAY, EVERYTHING ON THE DINGY WHITEWASH of the damp wall—all the stains, the fingerprints, the droppings left over by the flies, and the cobwebs—resembled a grandiose painting which evoked a myriad of associations, new and repeating forms as well as amazing, ghostlike shapes. Was it the murky drops of water trickling downward, was it the dampness of the wall itself, or was it rust from the reinforced steel which had made its way to the surface? It could also be mildew, moss, or lichens, which would thrive under the favorable conditions offered by such a tiny room. It was, at any rate, a strange and enticing world which enabled him to forget the shooting pain in his ribs. His heavy, weary eyes seemed to be searching in the filth for the reason, or one of the reasons, for his presence there. There must certainly be a reason somewhere in that somber and airless hole.

There seemed to be no one else present in the room, but he had been given orders not to turn around, and he followed them strictly.

At one point, he heard the door creak open. A slight breeze wafted over his body. Someone had entered. One, two, or several people. He could hear steps of varying intensity and felt for a moment that someone, one, two, or several people, were standing right behind him. He heard someone, one, two, or several people, breathing and then the steps fading away. They wandered off in the space he imagined to be behind his back. Somewhere not far away from him a light flashed. Tobacco smoke then spread through the room, a smell which seemed to revive him somewhat. He raised his head to catch a whiff of the smoke, his eyes followed the trickle of water in the corner of the room up to where the wall met the sloping ceiling. The more he looked upward, the less he could see prints of bare feet on the dingy, whitewashed surface. He stretched his neck a little, as if to open the pores of his weakened body to the fresh air which had entered the room through the open door. But this time, all he got was thicker smoke, which smothered him like a fist of cotton wool. He took a deep breath, inhaling smoke into the depths of his lungs, and now felt the shooting pain all the more.

The person who entered the room, or one of them, then departed. The door closed and the fresh air was gone. But the tobacco smoke became more and more intense. He could hear various steps in the distance once again, way behind his back. There were two of them, or perhaps three. Yet no one spoke a word, and although it was not absolutely still in the room, silence reigned heavily, as if beside a pond of stagnant water. The tobacco smoke brushed against his eyelashes. It singed them ever so slightly, calling for tears that had long gone dry. One of his fingers moved. He cast his eyes down at the bruised and blackened hands which were folded over his tightly pressed-together knees. He endeavored to move his fingers but to no avail. They remained flat and unmovable, like pieces of meat glued to his naked knees. Farther down toward his bare feet, he saw his toenails, discolored and far too long. Under the little toe of his left foot was a pool of dried blood which had formed around him. Its dark, ruddy hue, now with a tinge of pale yellow, made him quiver and struck a nerve on the ridge of his foot. The involuntary movement broke the crust on the recently coagulated blood, causing it to move—the snail which had taken refuge in the slimy shadow of his battered body. It moved.

"We always lean them against the wall. Why did we leave this one turned over on the floor here?" someone asked. Was it the one who had remained in the room or the echo of the other one who had just gone out? "Why don't we just get rid of him?" intoned the voice with the sentence he had heard so often recently. So there were two of them, or perhaps three or more. The cigarette smoke became thicker and filled his lungs.

"Let him shit his pants first," said one of them. The first, second, or third of them.

In fact he had just pissed his pants full, and the sentence suddenly made him aware of the strong burning sensation he had felt between his thighs, drenched with the sticky, salty urine. Perhaps he could move a little, just raise himself up enough to unstick the material from his bruised thighs. No, he wasn't allowed to. All movements were strictly watched, or to put it more exactly, forbidden. And thus he lay, cramped in the position he was in. Not daring to move his eyes from the pool of blood, he stared at a drop of urine which glided down his shinbone until it came to rest. The footstool with its wicker seat, crooked and shaky as it was, would betray any movement, so he had to keep his balance, remain immobile. But this presented no great difficulty because his body was stiff now anyway.

The door opened again and someone entered the room. Or someone left. He couldn't tell the difference. At a distance behind his back he could hear whispering but could not distinguish what was being said. They seemed to have reached an agreement. Perhaps something was going to happen. He listened attentively and endeavored to understand what had taken place. He heard paper and something like the scratching of a pencil. It sounded as if someone was signing a document, a signature at the end of a decree. An order had possibly come and they had to fill out forms or sign declarations. A badly worded sentence had been crossed out or a new one had to be added. They had reconsidered the matter.

He seemed to hear someone say, "Why don't we chain him to the wall?"

The glistening snail, bathed in its slime, had advanced somewhat. It had now reached the corner of the room, near the lower, dark-colored part of the wall where the footprints were the clearest. It was the only point that shone in the dark. Its shell rose like a Tower of Babel over the rotten floorboards, which held back some of the moisture oozing down the wall through the mildew. It advanced slowly, shining like a glow-worm under a spiral vault and without paying the slightest attention to what was happening around it. It was a volute among a thousand scarabs from some distant sphere, slithering forth in the ubiquitous mold and dampness, the sweat of the world, through nettles and over cold stones. But what was this gastropod hermaphrodite doing here in front of his aching eyes? From what dark hole had it emerged? And in what filthy corner of the wall did it intend to lay its eggs, only to become the ances-

THE SNAIL'S MARCH TOWARD THE LIGHT OF THE SUN

tor to generations of such beings slithering about in the very same filth, with the very same persistence and eternal patience, leaving behind them glowing trails, rays of slime betraying the paths taken, constantly inseminating, fertilizing itself and then depositing in the wall, from out of the right side of its head, the fruit of its hope?

In the slanting ceiling above him, right over the scarlet wounds on his now shaven skull, there was a tiny window which was never opened. The angle at which the rays of light fell upon the wall enabled him to tell the time of day, even to the exact hour on occasion. Now in the late afternoon, the rays fell obliquely through the window so that the light was at the very level of his eyes. It was like a shining white rectangle in which all the filth, stains, and streaks on the damp wall had miraculously vanished. This surface of light, which stemmed from and seemed to belong to another world, was like a fairy-tale garden with terrifying decorations and ornaments made of peeling whitewash, filth, fingerprints, and footprints, remnants of thousands of other lives right in front of him, constantly changing. There was almost no movement on the white surface. It was pure magic, a surrealist world of dreams and illusions, pure and unadorned, but containing all the hidden structures and impressions of a white painting in a frame. There, he could see his own little world and projected all of his dreams into it. There he called to mind everything real which he had not believed, or everything he had believed which had not been real. He could cast flashes of light, bolts of lightning, magic sparkles at it, transforming it into a thousand hues even more resplendent, otherwise hidden from his somber world.

The officer then entered the room, accompanied perhaps by someone else. One of them, at any rate, held a higher rank because he could sense the unease and hear the shifting movements in the little room. There was a clack of heels and then silence, broken at last by the officer with his rough and ominous voice:

"*Pomozhbog.*"

"*Pomozhbog!*"

Silence once more, and then the officer spoke out again:

"Has he moved?"

"No," was the reply.

"Is he still holding out?" he asked again.

"Yes," came the answer.

EQREM BASHA

"Has he been groaning?" he asked.

"Yes," they responded.

"Doesn't matter."

He could hear footsteps. Probably an inspection. The crack which accompanied the footsteps probably stemmed from the whip which the officer was wont to beat in the palm of his hand all day long.

"It stinks in here," he said.

"Let's set him against the other wall," someone proposed.

"He's not allowed to," was the frigid and sullen reply.

"He can't see much."

"Why do we lean all of them against the wall and this one with his face to it?"

"That's what the order says."

"Yes, sir."

The officer left the room, beating the whip in the palm of his hand as usual. The steps echoed behind him in the little room. Perhaps the others had left the room, too. One of them, two, or three.

For a long while he could hear only his own light breathing. He felt the biting pain in his ribs. Neither the big maps and pictures he had observed on the wall in front of him, nor the footprints, nor the traces left by the raindrops trickling in through the window down the wall through the mildew and the mold would be able to help him. It was evening now. His bones were awake and his wounds had opened. Only the trail left by the snail glistened now on the somber surface of the wall. The shell carried on upward toward the ceiling, toward the shining window which had now grown dark, and toward the sun, which had most certainly gone down by now.

In the shadow of his bare right foot, a little spider was silently weaving a web by attaching colorless strands between his foot and the wall. The web stretched to the leg of the stool. But he was too weary to watch it. His neck had become a rusty, ungreased axle. He watched the last drops of urine trickling down his thighs, causing the dry skin to itch. He saw the spider from the corner of his eye as it, unconcerned, continued to spin its web, a home built to last a thousand years. Given the state his body was in, it would at least be able to enjoy part of its retirement there.

The shining patch on the wall had vanished. There was darkness everywhere. Behind his back he heard a slight cough, enough to remind him of the presence of the night watchman.

THE SNAIL'S MARCH TOWARD THE LIGHT OF THE SUN

Night had fallen, just as it had so often before. The shining patch on the wall was gone and forgotten, and all the stains had vanished. No footprints could be seen and no noise was to be heard. The pain in his ribs had returned with a vengeance, as had the burning sensation in his chest, the ache in his back, and the numb feeling in his legs. The wall had closed in on him, like the curtain at the end of a play before the lights in the theater went on. The glistening snail had probably retreated into its shell or continued to march up the infinitely long wall in search of the sun.

Another day rose behind his back. The curtain opened and the performance began anew. The maps, the trickling water, the stains, the footprints, the lines and traces left over in the peeling whitewash appeared once again. The number of footprints had increased, or his eyesight, which had been weakened by the long night, could see only the part of the wall where they were most prevalent. What was definitely new was the network of slimy trails which the snail had left behind it during the night. And it was quite substantial. The wall now looked like the roof of a tent made of coarsely woven silk. Perhaps the poor snail had lost its way in the moonless night, or the setting of the sun had confused its sense of orientation. But nothing seemed to have stopped it. It covered the whole surface of the wall and was now stationary in the middle, unmoved, right at the level of his eyes. It was exhausted or was perhaps stopping momentarily to gather strength.

The shining rectangle was now somewhere behind his back. The light would later fall obliquely over his body and cast the shadow of his torso down toward his feet, reminding him of the paintings of Francis Bacon. Later, the rays would fall on his knees and on the lower, filthiest part of the wall, before they gradually rose toward the top and brought another day to its inevitable conclusion. But today there was something new: the network of trails which the snail had left behind glistening in the sun's rays like filigree had almost blinded his sight. It was so beautiful that it made him forget the shooting pain in his ribs and the wounds which covered his body. He could hardly hear the noise and the shuffling of feet behind his back. The breeze which wafted over him every time someone entered or left the room, the tobacco smoke, and the noise of papers and documents were all now insignificant, were no longer part of his world. The rectangle of light, now right in front of his eyes, sparkled like a waterfall of emeralds and diamonds. The light fractured into a whole spectrum and created one picture after another. In the corner, the snail, now revived, set forth on its definitive, straight, and unimpeded course toward the sunlight. The rays of light wandered upward and forced him to raise his head a little. All the while, the usual words were being exchanged behind his back:

"Is he holding out?"

"Yes."

"Has he moved?"

"No."

"Any groaning?"

"Yes."

"No matter. . . ."

Behind him, too, were footsteps shuffling back and forth, the beating of a whip in the palm of the officer's hand, the draft when the door opened, the smell of tobacco, a coming and going. Back and forth, paper and the scratching noise of a pencil. Steps, more steps. Someone came into the room, then another, a third. One of them went out and one came back in.

"Why do we lean all the others against the wall and this one with his face to it?" another one asked.

"Why don't we put him out of his misery?"

"I want him to shit his pants in horror first."

The usual, insignificant conversation. The drops of urine had dried up. No more followed. His breathing slowed down. He lay unmoved. The crooked and shaky footstool with its wicker seat and no back made no more noise, and the white rectangle with the bedazzling, glistening trails left behind by the snail filled him with new joy. He did not know when he had last eaten. Sure that he would hold out, he became awesomely courageous as he lay in front of the eternal wall.

"Kill me! What are you waiting for?" he might have said, had he had the strength. But it was of no importance. Beyond the glistening trails there was no more wall left. He felt something glide over his neck, something which gave him new strength and energy. He plunged into the silken cords, into the blinding light, and sank. Further and further he fell. What floor was he on now? From what heaven had he come? He could feel no ground under him.

THE SNAIL'S MARCH TOWARD THE LIGHT OF THE SUN

■ □ ■ □ ■

THE SECRET OF MY YOUTH

Mimoza Ahmeti

SHE HAD A RATHER CURIOUS NAME. THEY CALLED HER "EYES." I DON'T know whether she was given the name at birth, the time at which our parents give us names without taking our wishes into consideration, or whether she acquired it as a result of her big eyes. Whatever the case may be, it is true that those eyes of hers had a sense of perception much keener than what normal people could possibly imagine.

I had avoided those eyes for a long time. I could not help feeling a shudder down my spine when I heard someone whisper that her eyes sometimes underwent a perilous disfigurement. Quite normal people, for instance, had complained that they had seen themselves reflected in her eyes as a drop of water. Other people—serious, respectable, and admired individuals—had found themselves not reflected but grotesquely mutilated in her eyes.

No, I certainly did not want to see myself transformed into a monster in the eyes of a girl.

I had made a decision. Whatever should happen, I was resolved not to let myself be captured by her eyes. But . . . I had made that decision before ever being seen by them. And indeed, I *was* seen by them. Every time I try to avoid something, it homes in on me. Now there is nothing I desire more than to be captured by those two eyes, and this time totally.

I am presently convinced that everything beautiful on earth is an exception, an anomaly of sorts, toward which everything normal or average is attracted, in contradiction to its nature. Yes, and those all-possessing eyes could do nothing in essence but constitute an anomaly. They offered a precise reflection. Yes, I realize there is a dose of illusion in most human reflections. It is perhaps for this reason that knowledge as a process is so long and infinite whereas human existence is so short and ephemeral. Because the reflection in her eyes was so precise, many people were confused by them.

They were the most marvelous eyes I have ever seen in my whole life, the meeting of physical beauty and functional perfection. When I praised her eyes, that is, when I told her I loved her, she replied simply, "My eyes were not always like that. Experience has made them the way they are." She had never spoken to me of the particular quality of her glance. Perhaps she regarded it as a matter of course. And for her, it *was* one. But not for me.

I did not understand that when she observed something—a city, a flower, or a face, for example—a certain space in her eyes remained empty. The objects she observed did not always fill her gaze. It could very well happen that any object, however big it might seem, would leave a void. This unoccupied space in her eyes she often filled with blue sky or with dreams of the future. Such was her life.

I did not realize either that I was one of the rare human beings (though I doubt very much that I was alone in this capacity) to fill almost all the space in her eyes with my reflection. Almost. But almost is not the same as completely. There was a bit of space left over, a tiny bit of space, indeed so tiny that, had she wanted to, she could have filled that little corner with the reflection of a tree or a bird in the spring. But then, total bliss would have been beyond reach. It is only when her eyes were filled to the full with the person reflected in them, only when no space was left over in them that bliss could be attained. It was a strange game played between her eyes and her brain. Only now am I beginning to understand why she gazed so long at the sky. It filled her eyes to the full. She loved it.

I allowed my happiness to be jeopardized, the happiness of the two of us. I was incomplete. There was something missing in me, something that created a void, a tiny unfilled hole in the corner of her eye, but it was room enough for a reflection, and by no means the most unusual of reflections: the boon of happiness.

I could not understand, and I thought a lot about it later, why a girl with big, bright eyes should have made such a sacrifice. Perhaps it came about since, though I was incomplete, I was the most complete of all the incomplete persons she had known up to then. I was almost the one destined for her eyes. I was not completely the one, but almost. Do you understand now? Is it not terrible? It was simply a question of a little, tiny something missing but something which jeopardized everything.

And so she sacrificed herself. I did not realize that she was constantly reducing the size of her eyes solely to rid herself of that little hole which was always left over beside my refection. If only she had told me, if only she had mentioned the problem, I would have done battle with myself and, why not, done battle with the others to grow in her eyes, or at least to become sufficient. What a shame! I was insufficient, and I did not even know it!

I did not realize that she was reducing the size of her eyes for my sake. I noticed nothing to begin with. Perhaps she had not started reducing their size at the start since she was waiting for me to grow, to become big. It was later, when she had given up all hope of my growing, that I spotted the wrinkle in the corner of her eye, a fold in the muscle under the skin which disturbed me somehow.

The days passed. Her eyes became more and more disturbing for me, not in their beauty, but in the way she used them. They had withered, had decreased in size. And all the time, my love had withered and decreased in size. They were not the same two eyes I had caught a glance of at the start—eyes which people, both young and old, would gossip about at length. For me they had fallen into a morass of normality. Even worse. They had become devoid of all beauty. Deceptive eyes. That is the impression they made on me.

Anger began to take form within my breast. It looked as if she were making fun of me. And anyway, what significance could my love possibly have without her eyes? My words of reproach turned into insult. I could not understand why she put up with me. Her patience made me believe that I was right. I did not realize, as I now do, how rare, how extremely rare people were who could fill her eyes. I had attributed this rarity to my virtue. How ridiculous! She seemed to realize this and therefore put up with me. I was not the one, but I was almost the one. . . . So she put up with me.

The more I reproached her, the more patience she showed, the more her eyes withered and wrinkled, and the more their glance grew faint. Finally one evening I seized her by the shoulders and shook her in rage:

"You're lying, you're lying," I cried out. "You have ugly eyes, the ugliest eyes I have ever seen. Leave me alone! I've had enough!"

She was stupefied. As I shouted, her eyes slowly opened. To my surprise, they grew big and bright, penetrating and pure, just as they had been when I saw them for the first time, when . . . they were still free of me. I don't know why, but I was now speechless, with something stuck in my throat like a bone.

She gave no reply. She departed with eyes revived as I stood there benumbed from what I had done. No, not from what I had done. In reality, I was overwhelmed by the metamorphosis in her eyes. For one moment, a flash of lightning had illuminated the dark clouds of my doubts, a flash which proved lethal to my hardly profound conviction that I had been the cause of the withering and shrinking of her eyes, the most beautiful eyes on earth.

I called her name several times over. You will never believe how hard it was for me to call her by her name:

"Hey, Eyes! Come back, Eyes!"

But it was in vain. She did not return. Having turned her eyes away from me, I regained the place that I deserved in them. Soon thereafter my happiness dissipated. I had been almost complete but not complete. I was insufficient. The game played between her eyes and her brain was now interrupted.

She had no intention of returning. There was to be no more bliss. Perhaps there never had been. She had created it with hard work by wearing out, indeed by damaging, her eyes. Bliss is the only thing that we have still not learned to appreciate when it is bestowed upon us. A weakness? Perhaps. But because of it, I still feel human in my suffering. I suffer to become sufficient, to become perhaps something more.

Some people say that bliss is impossible, unreal. But I got very close and I know what it is, even though I did not succeed in mastering it. I believe that I can do it though. I want to take possession of bliss! Let them laugh at me all they want (laughing at someone else is often nothing more than a painful reflection of our own impotence). I want to attain the impossible. I want to be complete. I want to fill those eyes to the full. To attain total bliss.

This is the secret of my youth. One more reason for living.

■ □ ■ □ ■

THE PAIN OF A DISTANT WINTER

Teodor Laço

EACH AUTUMN, AS SOON AS THE DAYS BEGAN TO SHORTEN AND THE forests were covered with a blanket of golden leaves, the man began the long journey to his native village. It was a tiring journey at his age and in his precarious state of health. Neither his wife nor his daughters could understand what attracted, indeed compelled him to undertake the trip. He had begun making these visits at a time when, though still full of strength and vitality, he looked back with pain and regret at the long-gone days of his youth. Eleven years had passed since that day in March. It had been a muddy spring, the time of year before the leaves begin to bud under a clear sky, though one not without a hint of gray from the cold weather which still held sway. He had sold his mother's house for a ridiculous sum of money. It was an old cottage, so dilapidated that had it been left unoccupied for a year it would have collapsed. Up to that day, the spirit of his mother had kept it standing.

He left part of the money from the sale of the house with close relatives to pay for the upkeep of the grave and placed the rest in a savings account. When he married, he used it to buy some bedroom furniture and a refrigerator.

The sale had been a perfectly normal transaction, the kind made by dozens of people, so there was no reason for him to feel guilty. And yet, the muddy spring and the spending of the money had cast a shadow of culpability upon his soul. This feeling seemed to him to be due less to the sale of the house than to the death of his mother in his absence, for he had been unable to persuade the old woman to leave her village. He was still a bachelor at the time, living in cramped, rented quarters which he shared with another man, and thus was unable to invite his mother to live with him. But he could have organized his life differently. He could have married earlier, as his mother had wished, found an apartment, and invited the old woman to come and stay. Although she was strongly attached to her village, she was even more attached to the prospect of grandchildren. But no one can change the past, and so he had no choice but to come to terms with reality, which he did, though not without a certain regret for that which might have been. He imagined the long, lonely nights his mother must have spent in her room all alone, the unbroken silence that must have weighed more heavily upon her than the layer of snow upon the rooftops. The day he received the money—proof that the old house no longer belonged to his mother—he was filled with a sense of shame. . . . Over and over again he had plunged into a whirlpool of memories and endeavored to recall the events that first caused him such anguish. Strangely enough, though, his memory had never taken him back to that incident in his childhood of which he had only become aware during his trip the previous autumn.

It had been a long autumn, with an ever so gradual transformation from green to gold. There were still warm days like those at the beginning of summer. Indeed the illusion of summer was disturbed only by the autumnal colors and by the rarity of birds. He persuaded himself that, with such weather, it would be a sin to go by vehicle and decided to set out on foot. He had been walking for two hours and still felt full of energy. Like a child he delighted in taking shortcuts down untrodden paths through the long grass and bushes, not knowing if they would lead him back to the road. Resting on one of these paths in the shade of a lonesome fir tree which had not grown quite as high as the others, his childhood seemed to surface out of the past and sit down beside him. There it squatted, insolent and stubborn, and began telling him a story, like a long forgotten folktale. . . .

Once upon a time there was a little boy who was so in love with books that he quite forgot his childhood friends and their games. At night, when the light from his petroleum lamp began to waver and shadows appeared in the dark recesses of the room, as the fire in the hearth, singing an interminable song, crackled and hissed, characters would arise from the yellowing pages of his book and climb into his bed as if to warm themselves under the woolen covers. There was room for everyone under those covers and he could make them do whatever he wished. Robinson Crusoe could climb into a boat with Long John Silver and play hide-and-seek and other games. Slowly his eyelids would close and he would tremble in anticipation of the dreams that would make everything easy and possible. At dawn, he would abandon his night of wonder with a sigh of relief that he was now awake and, at the same time, with a sigh of regret at the knowledge that daytime would be so much more mundane than the adventures of the night.

Gradually, the boy began to read hunched over his books as if to devour every one of the letters that opened to him that wide world full of mystery. His mother scolded him, though only halfheartedly, for her son was at the top of his class in school and no good student could do without books. To please his mother, the boy would raise his head and hold the book at arm's length, but then the letters would begin to move like a trail of sluggish ants, causing the magic to vanish. He was ashamed that he was unable to keep his promise to his mother and, in order not to appear disobedient, stopped reading while lying on his stomach. His mother would perhaps notice that he no longer drew his eyes to the book but the book to his eyes.

The mother mentioned the problem to his teacher, who told her that he thought the boy was a little shortsighted. This disability could be remedied with a pair of eyeglasses, but to get them, she would have to take him into town to see a doctor. She had decided to wait until the snow melted, but by the middle of February, the boy had begun to suffer from severe headaches. She became frightened. It was clear to her that she could no longer wait until winter was over. She had made the trip from the village into town several times since becoming a widow and was not at all bothered by the cold weather or the solitude of the journey. The only obstacle was the snow, for every afternoon from sunset until late at night there would be a heavy snowfall that covered all traces of the paths. Every morning she rose early and heard herself say, "More snow again." She waited a whole week for the snow to stop, until she heard from other travelers that the road was clear.

The boy felt a chill run down his spine the moment the path led them into the semidarkness of the grove of fir trees. He shuddered and felt a knot in his stomach. The forest was large and little light penetrated this far. They were surrounded by silence, like that which reigned in the middle of the night when he waited for his dreams. But the silence was full of sounds, the incomprehensible language of nature, which not even the snow could muffle. It startled him, like a covey of partridges beating their wings in preparation for flight. He gasped for air, realizing that the panting which followed him like that of an invisible dog was his own. He glanced at his mother. Her cheeks were red with cold, but her face showed no trace of anxiety. He thought to himself that she probably could not hear the noises in the forest. Maybe there weren't any after all. But perhaps she was growing deaf in her old age, or perhaps the sounds were muffled by the black shawl that covered her ears.

Suddenly, he held his breath and bent forward. He thought he could hear a voice, different from the noises he had been hearing, a voice that sounded like a long howl of anxiety—a lament and a threat at the same time. The savage howl resounded down the bare face of the mountain, but the raging storm prevented him from determining quite what it was. "Did she hear it or not?" he wondered. His mother had stopped a bit farther on and had her back turned to him. He was not sure whether she was waiting or listening. He trudged on through the snow to reach her.

"Did you hear that?" he asked in a strangled voice. His mother took off her woolen gloves and stroked his hair, which was covered in melting ice.

"It was nothing," she replied.

"Take off your shawl and listen," he stammered.

The snow, melting under the warmth of her hand, trickled down his forehead.

"Perhaps it was a dog," she said.

"Or a wolf!" replied the boy.

"Wolves are afraid of people."

"But not in the winter. They are hungry now, roam in packs, and . . ."

He was about to add that in February the pack follows the she-wolf and that he had heard that a pack of wolves had once torn a hunter to pieces somewhere, but he thought better of it and bit his tongue. His mother must know as well as he that a pack of wolves might be coming their way. She seemed about to say or do something unpredictable. But she said nothing and did not move from the spot. Her face grew pale. There was not a shadow of doubt in his mind that the danger he had conjured up was now a reality and that the evil was approaching with awesome rapidity. Tales about wolves flashed through his mind and, horror-stricken, he rushed toward a fir tree standing alone in the middle of a clearing. Its trunk was thick and the first, half-withered branches were high up, but in his desperation he managed to heave himself up onto a solid branch. From there, he could see his tracks in the snow below, like those of some slithering reptile. His mother followed him, taking short steps. She leaned against the trunk of the fir tree, resting just long enough to get a grip on herself. He climbed up onto a higher branch, shaking snow down on her. She brushed the snow from her shoulders without looking up. He felt that she was unwilling to look at him. He climbed still higher. From there, he could see the wintry white expanses of the bare forest with a few dark spots here and there. He could not make out whether they were moving or not. If they were not moving, they were probably juniper bushes which had managed to shake off their covering of snow. Otherwise . . .

He listened again, and again heard the muffled howl borne by the wind through the dense fir tree. His mother heard nothing and remained silent. She looked so small and defenseless below him. He was ashamed of himself for having gone so far up and climbed back down to the withered branches below.

"Can you hear anything?" he asked again.

His mother gave no reply. She seemed to shrug.

"Come up here into the tree. It's safe here," he said.

"No, I can't," she replied.

The boy could hear the howling again, this time closer than ever. It was not echoing off the face of the mountain but coming straight out of the dark forest toward him.

"Try anyway," he insisted. "Here, can you reach my hand?"

"No, I'll never make it," said his mother. "Don't come down any farther. Stay where you are, Son."

On hearing this, the boy realized that his mother had no intention of moving from the tree trunk she was leaning against. Even if one of those miracles from fairy tales occurred and the cottage of a woodcutter with a solid door appeared before them, she would not budge from the tree. His hands and then his whole body began to freeze. His lips grew numb and his teeth started to chatter.

"Mother, my hands are freezing. Where are my gloves?" he asked.

"You dropped them when you ran off," she replied.

She rolled her gloves into a ball and threw them up to him. For a moment, neither of them spoke a word. Absolute silence reigned in the forest. The boy looked up and spotted a squirrel on a branch. It sat there proudly, like a host receiving guests. It stretched and shook its bushy tail, sending a shower of snow onto the boy's face. He wiped it off. The squirrel scurried farther up the tree, and a whole branchful of snow tumbled down onto his face. It scampered about, quite at home, with little concern for the huge, uninvited guest freezing in the cold down below who could not punish the little animal for the chilly dusting of snow on his hair and shoulders.

The wind came up again and he had the impression that it had taken the eerie howling off with it in the direction of the stream. The squirrel launched a pinecone it had been holding in its front paws. He climbed down slowly, with his cheeks aflame as if they had been slapped and with the tips of his fingers freezing and aching terribly. The stiffness in his limbs caused him such pain that tears welled up in his eyes. He could feel them turn to ice on his cheeks. He wanted to say something but was incapable of uttering a word. His mother took his hands and rubbed them in the snow until he could feel them again. Neither of them spoke a word.

They continued on toward town.

The boy never did learn whether they had been in great danger that day. He remained quieter than ever long afterward, roaming about the house as if searching for something he had lost, and his mother never brought the matter up again.

Many years passed before the anguish of the incident surfaced from the recesses of his mind where it had slumbered so long, finally to burgeon forth into conscious pain.

Every autumn when the leaves began to turn, he visited the grave of his mother in that distant village.

ANOTHER WINTER

Teodor Laço

ANOTHER LONG WINTER ARRIVED, WITH HEAVY SNOW THAT refused to melt away. At night, in the moonlight, the ice covering the swing out on the veranda sparkled like a scratched mirror, and the smooth frame cracked. It reminded him of that winter day he had been frightened of the wolves, a day that had vanished like a forgotten dream of which there remained only a lingering sense of uneasiness.

In fact, only a single spring, summer, autumn, and winter had passed since then.

That winter, something happened to his mother that was to be a source of wonder and mystery to him for years to come. People said that his mother was struck by a serious illness that winter, an illness from which she never completely recovered, but he thought otherwise. He was certain at the time that a miracle had taken place, one of those inexplicable events that seem impossible to us and make us laugh when we grow older. That day was the longest and most difficult day of his life. He knew that, from then on, nothing would ever again cause him such anguish, because his experiences as a doctor in the long years that followed had served to inure him to suffering and death.

He spoke to no one of what had transpired. Back then, he knew that if he told any of the adults what he had seen, they would simply smile condescendingly at him, as if to forgive him for talking such nonsense. After all, they themselves had fabricated many a fairy tale.

So he preferred to keep quiet. For many years he firmly believed that he had witnessed a miracle, and had he not become a doctor, he probably would have believed it his whole life.

On that distant winter afternoon, he was sitting in a corner of the living room, leaning on the windowsill. The sill was so broad that he used it as a table on which to do his homework. Snowflakes struck the window like sleepy butterflies. The logs on the fire hissed and crackled, and the cat snored in its winter quarters above the stone hearth. His mother slept in another corner of the room. She had fallen asleep right after lunch, and she was so still that he hardly dared turn the pages of his book. He watched as the path leading to the barn was slowly covered by snow and thought about his mother. His thoughts were sad ones because his mother had taken ill last autumn. Since then, she had shrunk so much that when she lay in bed with her legs drawn up, she looked like a little child. She staggered sometimes, and when this happened she would lean against the wall or against the door frame, as if nothing had happened, and give a little laugh to reassure him that she was all right. She didn't seem to realize that he was no longer so innocent that he would believe everything he was told. He already knew that adults were capable of dissimulation. His mother pretended she was well, and this charade saddened him more than her state of health. He never heard his mother complain. From time to time she told her friends that she saw stars before her eyes, but they simply replied that this was nothing unusual and that the same thing happened to them, too. His mother said this so nonchalantly that he assumed it was some sort of game for adults only, in which children for some reason were not allowed to take part. He thought it gave them pleasure to close their eyes, shake their heads back and forth, and see stars, twinkling as they do in the month of May.

He turned from time to time to watch his mother sleeping in the corner. She lay with her back to the fire, and a tuft of gray hair stuck out between the brown cap and the scarf she was wearing. He watched the fringe of the woolen blanket rise and fall with her breathing and was surprised at how tranquilly she slept. She never used to take a nap in the afternoon. He had heard that sleep was one of the best remedies for her condition.

A robin was pecking at the window. It beat its wings and rubbed its scarlet breast against the windowpane. He wanted to open the window and throw a few crumbs of bread out to the little bird but was afraid that the sash would creak and wake his mother from her sweet dreams, from the sleep that would help to cure her. . . .

He closed his reader carefully. Outside, the snow was still blowing and it was gradually getting dark. His mother would soon awaken and light the overhead lamp. She used to save fuel by lighting only the lamps with small wicks, but since her son had begun wearing glasses she lit the main lamp.

It was dark now and she would have to get up to feed the goats, he thought as he opened the window. The frightened robin flew off and disappeared into the falling snow. A gust of cold wind entered the room. His mother did not wake up. He glanced at her apprehensively and closed the window. The heavy snow continued to fall, blanketing the yard, the plum trees in the garden, the roofs of neighboring houses, and everything beyond them in a heavy mantle of silence. This great silence also seemed to harbor something unknown, something unfathomable and evil which might strike without warning. It seemed to him that this evil force had entered the room with the wind. He realized he was perspiring and assumed it must be because of the fire. Taking off his sweater, he went over to his mother's corner of the room. It must have been warm in the room because the cat had abandoned the heat of the hearth and had curled up on his mother's woolen blanket instead. His mother did not stir. Looking at her, the boy felt a twinge of pain in his chest. The cat and the fringes of the blanket seemed to be frozen, immobile, as if no one were breathing under them, though just a few minutes ago . . . He patted his mother on the shoulder. She did not move. The grayness of dusk reflected in the window, and the faint light which did penetrate the room veiled his mother's face in shadow. He placed his hand on her forehead. It was like touching an arabesque windowpane. His blood froze, but he told himself that perhaps she felt so cold because his hands were so hot. He shook her more forcefully. She had slept much longer than she usually did. She must wake up. It was time. The goats were bleating hungrily. It was time to light the lamp. In response to his shaking, she turned over on her side and remained there. The twilight fell on her gaunt face. The dark shadows withdrew and were replaced by reflections from the snow outside, pale and ghostly. His mother would not open her eyes. He didn't know what to do. He felt weak and helpless, as if he were once again a tiny infant.

TEODOR LAÇO

"Wake up, Mother," he begged, numb with fear.

She gave no answer.

"You've slept long enough," he cried and shook her again.

The cat was startled and scurried off, stepping on her wrinkled forehead with its paws as it did so, but even this did not wake her. The incomprehensible evil that had remained suspended all this time within the silence of the twilight now became tangible; the window blew open by itself and in rushed the cold winter wind. His heart contracted, and the anguish pent up inside him for so long was released and there was nothing to do but weep. But even his weeping was muffled. He had lost control of all his senses. Only his hands continued to move mechanically back and forth over his mother's face, over her gray hair, her cold forehead, her stiff eyelids which refused to open. He entreated her with cries, prayers, threats, and meaningless words. All he could remember later was the feeling of shrinking, of returning to his infancy. How long did it last? A moment or an hour? He would never know. His strength and reason had given way to a wave of anger at himself. His mother could not be dead. Death could not be so deaf, so mute. He recovered his faculties for a moment, bent down over his mother, and put his head to her breast. He thought he could hear, very faintly, the beating of her heart. Perhaps she had just fainted after all. He took a jug of water and sprinkled some over her face, but it remained motionless. He was overcome once more by a feeling of rage at his own helplessness, but in the midst of this rage a new thought occurred to him, like a lamp suddenly shining out of the darkness for those who have lost their way and abandoned all hope. He recalled his mother telling him about the time she was in the hospital in town, about the doctors and the miracles they performed. In our room, she had told him, there was an old woman at death's door. She was nearly gone when a doctor arrived, forced her mouth open, and gave her a glass of some syrup. The old woman came to and was able to leave the hospital on her own long before his mother was discharged.

In the darkness, the boy groped toward the cupboard where the sugar was kept. He filled a glass with water and quickly stirred in some sugar to make a sweet syrup.

Then he sat his mother up, supporting her with the pillows against the wall, and pried open her lips. They opened with surprising ease, as if his mother was acquiescing to his actions. He poured some syrup carefully into her mouth, taking care not to spill a drop. He saw a muscle jump in her neck—the first sign of recovery, he thought. Tears welled in his eyes as he whispered her name. It was a call from the heart, a call of pain and sorrow, a call of jubilation. Her mouth moved and, with her eyes still closed, she murmured, "Where am I?"

"You're here in your bed and I'm right here with you," he replied.

She opened her eyes, looking very weak and frightened. Only then did he realize that he should have acted sooner. He ran out to call the neighbors. Two women, friends of his mother, came in. One of them went to fetch Uncle Miti, a tall, thin, bespectacled man who was reputed to be the wisest elder in the village. Uncle Miti questioned him at length about what had happened, but he could find no explanation either.

"Make some coffee with lots of sugar!" the old man ordered. He caught sight of the glass on the windowsill, with some undissolved sugar still in the bottom. "Did you do this?" he asked as his glasses slipped down his nose.

The boy nodded.

"Your mother's guardian angel must have whispered in your ear," said Uncle Miti.

Uncle Miti was a religious man, and when the boy grew up he often recalled the old fellow's superstitious ways with a smile. He himself believed that it was only the miracle of his own will that had kept his mother alive. Throughout the spring and well into the summer, he would sit beside her in the afternoon and watch to make sure that the fringe on the blanket was rising and falling with her breaths. But the crisis did not reoccur. She seemed to adapt to her illness. She ate little and grew gradually thinner, and yet she could not keep still for a minute. People said she was like the branch of a cherry tree, constantly bending in the wind and yet never breaking.

When he became a doctor, he learned the explanation for this "miracle." His mother had fallen into a diabetic coma, in which one loses consciousness and for which doctors recommend sugar as a cure. Perhaps his mother's guardian angel really had whispered in his ear that winter's day so many years ago, and perhaps, despite all the scientific explanations, he really had witnessed a miracle.

TEODOR LAÇO

■ □ ■ □ ■

THE APPASSIONATA

Dritëro Agolli

I

I did not even tell Mira of my decision. She knew that the music conservatory was not the right place for me and that I might fail the year. She knew that the dean's office had met three times to discuss my work and had decided in the end to let me stay. Nonetheless, I wanted to leave at the beginning of the semester. In fact, I had never really wanted to attend at all, but my father insisted. He was impressed by the reputation of the National Institute of the Arts and considered it an excellent school. In his view, an artist in the family was proof of superior intelligence. Although he holds an important job, my father is still a child in many ways. Just as children tend to imitate their parents, my father enjoys imitating great intellectuals with their broad cultural horizons. He never misses a concert even though I know for sure that he knows nothing about music, especially symphonies, but he goes anyway. I find that irritating. Perhaps I'm wrong; perhaps my irritation is simply reverse snobbery. At times, when boredom gets to you, you can act like a snob and take a dislike to whatever your family does. I find many things my father does quite senseless, though they might well impress an outside observer. One time, he brought home a painter. He showed him through all the rooms of the apartment, and, standing before one of the walls, he ordered four paintings: landscapes and a still life. If he had found a good painter, I wouldn't have minded, but he came up with a real amateur.

So there was a possibility that I might fail the year. In desperation, I told my father that I intended to quit the conservatory because I did not like it. He turned as frigid as winter. Stuffing his hands in the pockets of his trousers, he paced back and forth in front of me. I sat there staring at the short legs hidden under his trousers. With a frown, he stroked his beard and then put his hands back in his pockets. I knew that all this posturing was designed to put psychological pressure on me.

"I am going to quit the conservatory," I declared, sitting back in the armchair.

He altered his pose to look hurt and then frowned again.

"When did you come up with this insane idea?" he asked.

I was irritated by his pompous tone.

"What's so insane about it? I've thought the whole thing through again and again," I countered, imitating his pomposity. He looked me in the eyes, as if to study my reaction, and said nothing for quite some time. It was a look designed to convey an impression of profound reasoning, but I knew it was nothing of the kind. An ironic smirk crossed my lips. My father stopped his pacing and halted in front of me.

I thought he was going to sit down in his armchair, but instead he headed for the front door, opened it slowly, went out, and shut it behind him. I remained alone in the apartment. Neither my mother nor my sister was at home. I took a book from the shelf and tried to calm my nerves by reading. A mixture of rain and snow was falling outside. It was February. The first few pages of the book contained a description of a fine sunny day. It was the story of a farm manager and a milkmaid, which I did not find overly impressive.

I closed the book and got up. Standing at the window watching the sleet fall, I recalled that my mother, who was from the countryside, had her own word for this mixture of rain and snow. She had only gone through primary school and had never had much education. She was a good-hearted soul, even now, although she had adopted some of my father's shortcomings. She too had become a bit vain and liked to boast about my father's work. She would confide in the neighbors some would-be secret about a staff member at one of the ministries, about goods for import and export, or about politics. It depressed me to see her influenced by my father's vanity. She considered him the most competent and most important man in town.

One evening I got angry with her. Someone had phoned to talk to my father. My mother answered:

"Mr. Reufi is not available at the moment. May I transmit a message?" I was not so upset about the "transmit a message" as about the "Mr. Reufi."

"Aren't you pushing it a bit, Mother?" I said with a gesture of impatience.

"What do you mean?"

"Mr. Reufi," I jeered.

"Your father is an important figure, Arthur," she replied.

I disliked the pretentiousness of the name Arthur, too. It had been my father's choice.

I stood at the window, looking down at the wet boulevard. People were rushing in all directions, huddled under their umbrellas. I could hear the rain gushing from our balcony onto the pavement below.

The radio was playing the *Appassionata*. I loved that piece. It never failed to move me, though I am certainly no composer myself.

The next day I was intending to go to the dean's office and tell him that I was quitting the conservatory. I have no talent for music. I was majoring in composition, and to be a composer means to be a creator, and I am not a creator of music. My father's vanity had made me an object of ridicule among the students. Mira, too, knew that they made fun of me. She is studying piano and holds the promise of becoming a good pianist. But what promise do I hold? None. A composer? I am thoroughly convinced that all possible combinations of keys have already been discovered and used, and that there are no new ones to be found. Thousands and thousands of songs, symphonies, sonatas, études, operas, operettas, and cantatas resound all over the continent. A universe of sounds had already been created and to enter this universe you needed the right uniform. I had simply not found the uniform. Mira had. So had Burhan. But I haven't. I could build a bridge or mount a turbine. Why should I have to compose a symphony or even a song?

I thought of going to the women's residence and of telling Mira that I was quitting the conservatory. I was sure that she would approve of my decision, and be relieved and happy about it. She would no longer have to listen to the others making fun of me or asking me with a smirk, "How many keys are there between do and ti, Arthur?"

But who knew what Mira was doing now at the residence? Perhaps she was wading through a history of operatic music from Verdi to Wagner to coach the others. Go ahead and coach them, Mira! I've read books about Verdi and Wagner, too, but not to be able to parrot the information. I just read them for interest. Like history books. It's funny, isn't it?

With Mira on my mind, I was about to go out when I heard my father's footsteps.

2

My father took his coat off, hung it up in the hall, and entered the room. He had a somber look on his face.

"Where are you going?" he asked.

"I was just going out to meet a friend!"

"Sit down for a moment," he said, motioning to a chair.

I sat down. He took a packet of cigarettes and a lighter out of his waistcoat pocket. I could smell the tobacco and the lighter fluid.

"Every stage of life," he said, "is subject to many factors."

I could feel the word *but* on its way and decided to counterattack: "Factors can change and improve."

He raised his eyes under their thick eyebrows and gave a big laugh, which I was not expecting. He took out his striped handkerchief and wiped his eyes. Lowering his head, he placed the handkerchief back into his pocket.

"Very clever," he murmured, taking his hand out of his pocket.

I rose to my feet.

"Sorry, Father, but my friends are waiting for me."

He made an impatient gesture which betrayed his anger.

"Sit down!" he ordered.

I hesitated for a moment on my long legs and sat down.

"You have been hiding things from me," he said gravely.

"I told you frankly enough that I am quitting the conservatory."

"You are hiding things from me, Son," he repeated with a note of displeasure in his voice. "I succeeded in getting you into the National Institute of the Arts without your going through the entrance exams. You entered on the recommendation of influential people. A whole ministry acted on your behalf. And now, after a mere five months, you intend to trample on everything we have done, all the favors and assistance. If my colleagues find out what you have decided to do, they will be put in a very awkward position. And it will be extremely embarrassing for me, your father. I inquired at the dean's office, and they assured me that you had talent but that you were wasting your time on matters incompatible with your studies, a fact which I find revolting."

I gave my father a pitying look. His forehead was perspiring. Drops of sweat had formed around his mouth and under his nose, at the edge of his moustache. What he said was true.

"Revolting!" he shouted.

"I'm surprised," I said.

"You have no reason to be surprised! Revolting! Now they tell me that your thoughts are not concentrated on your studies, your sonatas or solfeggios or whatever you call them, but on the fair sex."

It was obvious that my father was furious. He stammered and repeated himself, but I was still not too sure where he was leading.

"The fair sex?" I asked.

"The sair fex! Girls!" he shouted, bathed in sweat and foaming at the mouth.

I couldn't keep a straight face. I got up and laughed out loud. In his hysteria, my father had committed one of his spoonerisms.

"Shut up and sit down!" he ordered. "Revolting, I tell you! It's all this television! This hippie generation! Aping everything from the West! East and West together!"

I bit the back of my hand to keep from laughing again.

"Get that hand away from your mouth!" my father shouted and jumped up.

I had to keep my hand in front of my mouth to prevent myself from giggling. My father grabbed my arm. My giggling stopped at once.

"You hippie!" he cried, and turned his back on me.

He stopped at the door, turned toward me, and added in a calmer voice, "This girl you've been seeing at the conservatory—Mira is her name, isn't it? All right. Do whatever you want! Go ahead and concentrate on the girls and forget your solfeggios and studies. You'll see what a mire this Mira is going to leave you in." With this, he left the room and stomped down the hallway.

All alone, I was indignant that Mira's name had been drawn into the matter. Why should she be involved?

3

The next day I was at the conservatory early in the morning. The first two hours were taken up by our third lesson in the basic principles of aesthetics. These lessons I enjoyed because they were less monotonous than the rest. It should have been the other way around, but as I had no talent for music itself, I didn't enjoy the practical courses at all. The basic principles of aesthetics interested me. In fact, Mira suggested that I should change my major and become an art critic. But this seemed to be an arduous field, too. What I was aiming at was the Faculty of Engineering. What would I gain by becoming an art critic? Even if I did have the talent for it, it did not interest me sufficiently. I could have written reviews on different composers for the cultural periodical *Drita,* and they would have turned up their noses at me whenever we met at the Writers' and Artists' Union. Why bother? I would rather construct apartment buildings or dams anyway! And I have no talent for music! My father is obsessed with the idea that I am a musical genius.

Pale and worn out, I met Burhan and Mira in class. They asked if I had been ill, but I told them it was simply a lack of sleep. It was during class that I whispered to Burhan, "I've decided to quit the conservatory."

Burhan stopped writing in the thick notebook in front of him.

"You would be better off to wait until the end of the semester. There are only three or four more exams to go," he said.

"No! I'm leaving now," I replied.

"You shouldn't. Wait until the end of the year. After the summer break you can register at the university. I think you've made the right decision. Everyone has to find his own niche in life. But just wait another three months," Burhan advised.

I liked Burhan. He was a sensible, levelheaded person. He never learned anything by heart but approached everything with logic and reason. We all liked him. He may have been a bit conservative. He disliked all the flirting between the sexes at the conservatory and believed that love had to wait until after the conclusion of a mission undertaken. Strangely enough, he never took me to task for being in love with Mira, nor did he reproach her for being with me. He spent a lot of time with us and even made me jealous on occasion! I had the impression that he was in love with Mira, too, but I never let my jealousy show. Nor did I say anything to Mira.

"I can't wait anymore! I'm not staying at the conservatory any longer. Don't you see that I'm making a fool of myself, Burhan?" I said.

Burhan said nothing. He began taking notes again. I pretended to be listening to the professor and continued talking to Burhan from time to time. The professor noticed us but was a lenient man and said nothing. I tore a page out of my notebook and wrote a couple of lines: "Mira, I've decided to quit the conservatory." When I finished writing, I passed the note to Mira, who sat on the bench behind us.

A few moments later, she stuffed a slip of paper into my pocket. I opened it. "Good idea," it read.

Although her response was objective enough, it irritated me. It seemed to me that she was waiting for me to leave so that she would not be embarrassed by my bad marks and my lack of talent. "Obviously," I said to myself, "Mira is glad to get rid of me. She is going to leave me and fall in love with Burhan, if she hasn't already." I was furious at all women. I was also furious at Burhan, sitting at my side. Simmering with wrath, I said nothing more until the end of class. "At the Faculty of Engineering I could be the best student and here I'm the worst," I thought to myself, my anger extending now to my father. Why this pretentious fascination with music when he knew absolutely nothing about it? He was completely ignorant in this field. Mr. Reufi, the music lover. What a clown! It saddened me to be calling my own father a clown. He had done so much for me and here I was calling him that. It was I who was the clown.

At that moment the bell rang. Noise filled the auditorium and the three of us went out. I walked along with my head lowered, hoping to avoid having to talk to anyone. I stuffed my hands in my pockets and stared at my legs, which were advancing mechanically.

The three of us stopped by the window. The courtyard in front of the conservatory was wet with the February rain. Neither Burhan nor Mira spoke. They, too, gazed out onto the courtyard. As we stood there, a cream-colored car drove up. It swung around and parked in front of the entrance. I recognized it as my father's limousine. Yes! A moment later I saw my father himself descend from the vehicle. Dressed in a heavy winter coat and a black hat, he began climbing the stone staircase. He mounted slowly, step by step, with the air of an important figure. My friends recognized him, too.

"Look, there's Mr. Reufi!" cried Burhan and looked at me.

"Yes, it's my father all right," I said calmly and turned away from the window. Mira followed me.

"Are you going to go and see him?" she inquired.

"Why should I bother? I see him at home every day," I replied coldly.

"Do you love your father, Arthur?" she asked.

"What a question!" I countered.

"I asked only because whenever he comes here you look distressed," she noted.

"The shadow of my father distresses me," I added.

"What does he think of your leaving the conservatory?" she asked.

"He understands," I lied and regretted the irony in my voice. I did not want Mira to know about the chilly relations between my father and me, but she seemed not to notice that anything was amiss.

The bell rang and we returned to class.

4

Burhan and Mira accompanied me almost all the way back home and were just as uneasy as I. These were my last days at the conservatory. Although it was my own wish to leave, my heart ached at the thought of no longer seeing my friends, the auditorium, the staircase. If I had had but one ounce of inclination, if not to say talent, for music, I would not have left. But I knew that I had been in that temple of the muses too long already. There were others who knew they had neither the inclination nor the talent and yet continued to follow the herd. They gravitated inertly toward the more talented students, spent all their time with them, and considered themselves talented. They would adopt the attitudes and views of the gifted students and turn up their noses skeptically at what others were doing in art. They were snobs. Snobs for me are people who play the part of apes, or apes who play the part of people. That is something I simply cannot do. I could turn up my nose at others, but I refuse to do so.

"If you leave now, you are going to be bored stiff at home until the new school year begins. You can't start university in midsemester," said Burhan.

Mira was listening to him. She turned to me and waited to hear what answer I would give. I was slightly offended at the idea that Burhan thought I would sit at home or loiter around in the streets doing nothing. He thought that since my father had an important position I would be choosy and would refuse to accept just any job. I turned toward him, sensing from his expression that I must look worn out.

"I don't intend to wait for the new school year to begin," I said.

"Well, what are you going to do then?" he asked.

"I am going to get a job in a factory. I like machine and tractor plants, for instance."

Burhan stopped. He gave no sign of surprise, but I knew that he did not believe a word I was saying.

"Mr. Reufi won't let you," he said.

I was not too pleased by Burhan's view of my father. I do argue with my father, but I don't accuse him of faults he doesn't have. What made Burhan think that my father wouldn't let me work in a factory?

"Look, Burhan, my father wasn't born with a silver spoon in his mouth," I said.

"Sorry," replied Burhan. "What I meant was that your father wants you to continue your studies, and he won't be too pleased at the idea of your getting a job instead of going to university."

"Yes, that's what he meant," Mira broke in placatingly.

I looked at her, thinking, "Why does she always have to take Burhan's side?"

I was hoping that he would leave so that I could be alone with Mira. "Burhan is so thick! Why doesn't he leave the two of us alone? What if I wanted to hold her hand or even kiss her? What is he waiting for? He's a good friend, but still . . ."

Burhan seemed to understand that his presence bothered me and, as we were near my home, said he had to be off because he had to meet a friend.

I remained alone with Mira. Slender and wrapped in her blue coat, she walked beside me in silence. The wet street and the dampness in the air seemed to have penetrated the marrow of her bones. From time to time she shivered and huddled close to me as if in search of warmth.

"Are you cold, Mira?" I asked.

"A bit," she replied.

"Mira, I am going to quit the conservatory, but that doesn't mean that we won't see one another," I said, taking her hand. Her little fingers were lost in my palm. They were cold and I squeezed them. I could feel a current of warmth and sweetness pass through my body. Mira lowered her head. Her black hair covered one eye and half of her lovely face. She was the only girl I had ever loved. She had come to the conservatory from Korça, and we had met in the very first days of the school year. Of course she could not know at the time that I had no talent for music. I may have looked talented and sensitive, but something was lacking in me. I didn't have the soul of a musician. And yet I was sure she would love me even if she discovered my lack of talent.

It pained her to hear the others making fun of my weakness in music. Sometimes she would go red in the face and become furious. But she loved me anyway.

We heard footsteps behind us. It was my father in his heavy coat and black hat. He caught up to us and stopped. Mira cowered behind me. I could sense her quivering.

"So you are out for a walk instead of at your studies I see," he said in a huff.

"Our classes have just finished," I replied coldly.

My father was silent for a moment. He gave us a look and then, backing off slowly, departed with a solemn stride.

"I didn't know what to do!" said Mira slowly.

"There's no reason to be afraid," I said.

"Your father is an imposing figure."

"He plays the part professionally. He considers us and everyone else his subordinates," I said.

"How can you say that about your father, Arthur?" Mira chided.

"I was just joking," I said, giving a laugh.

I walked Mira to the bus station and then returned home.

My parents were having lunch. I sat down and watched the movements of their spoons. My father was chewing, and his lips were making a noise like someone treading on muddy ground.

"You're back?" he said without raising his head.

"I'm back," I replied.

"So you're back!" he repeated.

"Yes, I'm back," I said again.

My mother interjected,

"Do you want something to eat, Arthur?"

"All right," I replied.

From their attitude I saw that they had been talking about me. My father had no doubt been playing the prosecution and my mother had been taking the defense.

She loaded my plate with food, and I went to sit down at my father's side, the two of us munching away, he loudly and I quietly.

"Are you tired?" my father asked.

"Yes, I am," I responded, my eyes fixed on my plate and the spoon in my hand.

"Tired of walking the streets," he said, wiping his mouth with a napkin.

"You're right, and I'm also tired of hearing your accusations," I answered calmly.

My father rose from the table, his cheeks scarlet. He did not like my answer, although I had not contradicted him.

"You're wasting your valuable time with that little tramp. You may have talent for women but no talent for music," he uttered, gradually bringing the tone of his deep voice to a crescendo.

"Enough now. Let him eat his meal in peace!" my mother broke in.

"All right, I should leave him alone, should I?" said my father sarcastically.

I ignored him and continued to eat. It infuriated him to see me eating calmly while he was so upset.

Approaching the table, he seized my spoon and hurled it to the floor.

"I am talking to you, and you sit there eating your lunch as if nothing had happened!"

I could feel his heavy breathing on the back of my neck. I rose and said, "I'm sorry."

My father gave no reply, nor did my mother. I stood in front of him defiantly. I could feel that I was paling.

He stood in front of me for a moment, then turned and went off into his bedroom. My mother and I remained in the kitchen. I could not bring myself to sit down again. I stood staring at the blank wall for several moments. It was like the sensation I had at the conservatory after an exam. I was the last student to be examined. All the others had gone. The students had left and the professor was gone, too. I stood there clutching my notebook and staring. There, face-to-face with the auditorium wall, I felt my total defeat, the futility of all my efforts. I became aware that my presence in that auditorium was a huge mistake. The longer I stayed, the more I would suffer. I would suffer all my life from an inferiority complex, from a feeling of being a mediocrity, a boor. On graduation I would join the ranks of those with diplomas of higher education who are neither specialists nor intellectuals. I would become a statistic in a yearbook and nothing more. I did not want to be a simple statistic. I stared at the wall with the notebook in my hand and began to shiver. Suddenly I felt relieved, relieved to have found myself. "This is not my road in life," I said. "There are other roads." I put the notebook in my pocket and departed. It was that moment I recalled as I stood in the kitchen, as my mother sat silently at the table, as my food remained uneaten on the plate, and as Mira sat at home at the women's residence.

"Listen to your father," said my mother. "He knows what he's talking about."

I sat down on a chair. It was only then that I became aware of what my mother was saying.

"I don't want to become a statistic!" I said.

My mother stared at me: "A statistic?"

"A statistic!" I repeated.

She had no idea what I meant.

5

I did not return to the conservatory the next day. I lay on the couch with my hands behind my head, staring at the ceiling, daydreaming. The other students were now in their second class. Mira was sitting on a bench and writing. Burhan, with his pronounced jaw, was sitting behind her, taking copious notes. My father was at the office perusing important documents about important meetings of concern to the division he headed. They all say that he works hard and expects everyone else to do the same. I have no doubt about that. My father is a hard and conscientious worker all right. I have seen him work both at home and at the office. Whenever he has a report to write he is all keyed up like a child. He writes, gnaws nervously at his pencil, gets up, sits down. He is daring in his criticism. He once criticized his superior, Shemsedin, for wasting money on building a public library for a small town, a building which, as my father predicted, became outdated within ten years and had to be rebuilt. My father was right, I know, but what would Mira be thinking now? She would perhaps be thinking that I would never return to the conservatory. Maybe the time had come for us to go our separate ways. I would become an engineer and she would be a musician. We would have nothing in common. Unless of course I married her. My wife the musician. I gave a loud laugh, and my mother came into the room.

"What's wrong, Arthur? Why are you crying?" she asked anxiously.

She stood beside me and stroked my forehead, saying calmly, "Leave the conservatory, Son. You're just torturing yourself," and took out a handkerchief to wipe a tear off my cheek.

She smiled.

"How you frightened me! I haven't heard you cry since you were a child."

"I was laughing, Mother."

"That was no laugh," she said and left the room.

I trembled in confusion. I am not superstitious but was taken by an ominous foreboding. "It was true," I said to myself, "I had been crying."

At that moment the telephone rang. My mother went to answer.

"Yes? Mr. Reufi? No, Mr. Reufi has no meeting today. He will be back at two thirty this afternoon. Where are you calling from? The conservatory. I'll give him your message. All right," she said and hung up.

I studied the expression on her face.

"You see, Mother? Mr. Reufi! Why do you call him Mr. Reufi on the phone? At home you just call him Demo."

She looked at me tenderly.

"Everyone calls him Mr. Reufi on the phone. It's just become a habit."

"Well, it's a bad habit."

"But tell me, Arthur, why do you want to quit the conservatory?"

"I simply have no talent for music, Mother," I said earnestly.

"You have no talent? And what about Burhan, that simpleton? You are surely more talented than he is. Isn't there some other reason? Your father said you have been chasing girls and neglecting your studies and that was why you wanted to quit."

"That isn't true. I simply have no ear for music."

"Don't be silly! Burhan has sandals for ears. Why should he be any better?" she asked.

I smiled.

"What are you smiling at?" she asked. "You're an intelligent boy. Why shouldn't you finish your studies at the conservatory?"

"What would you prefer, Mother? For me to have a prestigious job and be worse than everyone else or to have a less impressive job and be just as good as everyone else?"

My mother shook her head.

"For you to be just as good as the others," she admitted quietly.

Just then, the front door opened and I caught sight of my father's hat and black coat. He shut the door quietly behind him and entered the room, looking out toward the balcony. He took off his coat and hat and sat down on a chair without saying a word. Giving me a quick glance, he turned to my mother.

"Did anyone phone for me?"

"The conservatory," she replied.

"About *him*," he muttered, pointing to me.

"I don't know," said my mother.

"But *I* do," he said, turning toward me. "So, you were not at the conservatory today, young man. You prefer to spend the day in bed or whatever it is you've been doing."

"God," I thought to myself, "he is going to start up with that 'whatever' business again."

"All right, all right," he said, turning to my mother. "Let's have lunch."

A heavy silence fell on the room, broken only by the clatter of plates and cutlery. Our arguments always seem to be preceded by an overture of clattering plates and cutlery.

"So," said my father, sitting down to the table, "we have to waste our time dealing with our son's escapades, as if we didn't have enough work on our hands. We get to follow his adventures at the dean's office and the rectorate. A fine repayment for all we've done for him!"

I thought it was best not to say anything.

"Eat your meal, Demo," said my mother.

"It's like poison. I feel like I'm eating some well-prepared poison."

My mother gave me a frightened look.

"I have been told a lot of things about this young man. They say he is supposed to be capable, talented. But unused talent is the same as no talent at all. Has he been given an opportunity to use his talent? Yes. It is not the government's fault. I have been told that he is not attending classes. He has been chasing after one of those miniskirts, one of those wiggling, giggling bits of skirt," he shouted, rising to imitate a young girl.

This was one of the funniest scenes ever to have taken place in our house, but I was careful not to laugh. My mother gave a laugh though and was repaid with an angry glance as he sat down again. He had not yet touched his food.

"He has taken up with one of those girls I was talking about, has abandoned his studies, and now he wants to quit the conservatory altogether. The dean's office and the rectorate should never have allowed girls like that into the conservatory. It's unbelievable!"

"Don't insult a nice girl," I interrupted dryly. My father turned to me, his heavy eyebrows frowning over eyes sparkling with fury.

"We often defend those who are unworthy of defense in order to defend ourselves. That is what you are doing," he said.

"We often give others the blame to save our own skin. You're blaming her to defend me because things have to be the way you want them to be. There is a fundamental error in your thinking. I already told you. I have recognized the fact that I have no talent for music. It was clear to me from the very start that this road is not taking me where I want to go. If I continue down it right to the end, I will have to go all the way back eventually, and that will make it all the more difficult for me. So I'd rather choose another road now. You think it's because of her? Well, let me tell you"—I began to tremble—"I don't need you to tell me what to do at every step I take in life. It was you who pointed me down that road and I obeyed. But it was a mistake. Now I'm taking my own road. And I don't need you anymore."

My father stared at me, rose to his feet, and began pacing back and forth. Steam was still rising from the dishes heaped with food. Then he stopped and looked at me as if I were a complete stranger.

"Me telling you what to do?" he murmured. "You have learned some strange ideas. Is that the way all young people think nowadays? The right road, self-knowledge, awareness of your talents, of your limitations. Do you think you have justified yourself and convinced me?"

He sat down and took up his spoon, saying no more. I could hear it clattering in the soup dish.

6

Several days passed. I did not return to the conservatory. My father reported to the dean's office that I was ill. I had made up my mind not to go back and had even applied for a job at the tractor plant until the start of the next academic year. The head of personnel said I could start work the following week. I had learned how to use a lathe during extracurricular production work at secondary school. I did not tell my father about my applying for a factory job because I was afraid he would stop me.

I spent those days at home reading. I was also teaching myself English, poring through elementary texts and noting all the words of vocabulary I didn't know. I spoke the texts out loud and listened to lessons on the tape recorder my father had bought for me. I had several plans. I wanted to start with English and then learn French, too. Two languages are enough. Any more than that is a waste of time unless you are a linguist.

While I was reading in my room, my mother came in and told me that Burhan wanted to talk to me.

"Is he on the phone?" I asked.

"No, he's at the door," she replied.

I ran out. He was standing in the doorway with an umbrella in his hand.

"Hi, Burhan!"

He entered slowly with his hand to his chin. He walked down the hall to my room silently and somberly.

He sat down in the armchair across from me.

"What's new at the conservatory?" I asked.

"Nothing much. Have you decided to quit for good?"

"Yes, I've made my decision, Burhan."

He rubbed his forehead and crossed his legs.

"Mira wanted to come, but she couldn't leave her father alone," Burhan added.

"What, Mira's father is in town?" I asked.

He did not answer immediately. He looked over at the tape recorder on the table and at my English course.

"You're studying?" he asked.

"A little bit," I replied.

"The dean's office asked him to come," said Burhan.

"Why?"

"It's hard to explain. It's a bit complicated. They want to expel Mira from the conservatory," stated Burhan.

I jumped.

"Expel her?"

"It's complicated, Arthur."

"You already said that. Tell me what happened?" I shouted, upset at Burhan's composure.

"They say she's a bad influence on the male students," he replied.

I blushed. It was only with me that Mira was on more than just friendly terms.

"What male students?"

"You! They say she is responsible for your neglecting your studies and quitting the conservatory. Now they want to expel her to save you," explained Burhan.

I jumped up angrily.

"What a senseless sacrifice!" I said.

He looked at me quizzically, so I explained, "They want to sacrifice someone else to save me? In history there is a story about a woman who sacrificed herself for an ideal. She was locked in behind four walls and sacrificed her happiness for the sake of her husband, who was very talented. But it was at least her own choice. They want

THE APPASSIONATA

131

to sacrifice Mira for me, and I don't even have any talent. I am only the son of a director. . . ."

I went on at length, expounding ideas which had been pent up within me for a long time. Burhan listened patiently with his jaw resting in the palm of his hand.

I thought of my father. There was another aspect to his move against Mira. He did not want me to marry her and raise a family without finishing my studies and having a professional career first. He saw my relationship with her as the prelude to marriage. To save me from throwing away my future, he would sacrifice Mira by separating us. The motives were complex indeed!

"They called Mira's father to tell him about his daughter," Burhan said. "He was devastated. Poor man, he was completely confused. At first they gave Mira a choice: stop seeing you or be expelled. Then they changed their minds and decided to expel her no matter what. Her father has come to take her home. What do you say?"

Burhan studied me, waiting for me to reply.

"They can't do this to her! They can't expel her!" I cried.

"That's what I thought too, but I am afraid they have, Arthur. Your father's been to the dean's office several times," he added.

I was red with shame and rage. My fingers moved nervously back and forth over my knees.

"So what do we do?" I said to Burhan.

He was silent.

I still did not want to hear anyone criticize my father. Burhan was my friend, but I would not let even him speak badly of my father. Yet of course Burhan was right. It must have been my father who made them expel Mira from the conservatory. Only now did I begin to think about my father's conversations and his criticism of her and of girls he considered a bad influence. But I did not want Burhan to discover the full truth.

"Listen, Burhan. My father wouldn't do a thing like that," I said, blushing at my own lie. I hoped he would not see through it. "Would my father go that far? Would a man known at work for his honesty descend to such depths," I wondered as Burhan, wise, kind Burhan, sat in front of me.

"I have my doubts, Arthur. Don't misunderstand me. I respect Mr. Reufi, but he is the one responsible for this. He's the only one in a position to apply that kind of pressure. He is a powerful person, Arthur, and is capable of doing it . . . ," said Burhan thoughtfully.

"Why such accusations?" I broke in.

He frowned. I realized that he was offended.

"What do you mean 'accusations'? The future of an individual is at stake. Should we just look the other way?" he said slowly, containing his anger. I blushed. His words were convincing. More convincing than those of my father.

"You have the right to believe whatever you want. Everyone does," I replied evasively. Burhan rose to his feet.

"Don't go yet," I pleaded.

"I must go," he replied coldly. "Sorry to have bothered you. Go back to your books!" He picked up his umbrella and left without saying another word.

Alone in my room, I realized what he meant. Someone's future was being destroyed on my account, and I was sitting here studying English. I should have run after him and gone to see Mira.

I threw on my coat and rushed down the stairs.

My mother called after me, "Arthur, where are you going?"

I ran and ran.

7

I never caught up to Burhan. I took a bus going toward the women's residence. I thought of nothing but Mira all the way. I blamed my father, but I still could not believe that Mira would be expelled from the conservatory. The misunderstanding had to be cleared up. One accusation was not enough to decide someone's fate.

I got off the bus and walked up the lane that led to the residence. I had walked up this lane many times with and without Mira. The whole neighborhood was verdant on those spring evenings, and the air was filled with the sound of girls laughing, talking, and singing the occasional song. Now on this cold and rainy February day, it was quieter.

At the entrance stood a short man with a brimmed hat. He was waiting for someone. He was smoking a cigarette and had his eyes fixed on the building. I was sure it was Mira's father, though I had never actually seen him before. He studied me and then turned away and began to walk down toward the little courtyard.

He was a few meters away when I went up to the doorman and asked him to call Mira. He nodded in silence and came out of his booth. Quite unexpectedly he turned toward me and said, "Her father is waiting for her, too."

"Is that right?" I said and looked over at the man pacing back and forth with his eyes fixed on the ground and a cigarette in his mouth. I was tempted to introduce myself, but I decided to wait for Mira. He looked like a wise man but one who was carrying a heavy burden.

At that moment, Mira appeared in the little garden, dressed in her blue coat. I glanced toward the man. When he realized that I, too, was waiting for her, he appeared to shrink, as if he were trying to withdraw into his cream-colored duffle coat.

Mira gave me her hand. There was a gleam in her eyes despite the sadness of her expression. She seemed to think I was bringing good news.

"My father is here, too," she murmured and approached him timidly.

"Let's go, Daughter," he said in a shrill, quivering voice.

I stood a little apart from them. Mira turned toward me and said to her father, "This is a friend of mine from the conservatory."

We shook hands. He looked at me with his little eyes as if wondering, "Is he the one?" But he retained his composure.

We started off down the lane. Where were we going? What should I say to him? How could I find out what had been said at the dean's office? What could I do to speak to Mira alone? It would be difficult to separate the two of them.

As we were walking, he suddenly asked me, "Whose son are you?"

"I live in Tirana, but my parents are from Korça. My father moved to Tirana right after the liberation."

"Is that so? What is your father's name?"

"Demosten Reufi," I replied.

"Really? You are Demosten's son?" he exclaimed.

"Do you know him?"

"And how! We were in the same battalion during the war. Good old Demosten!" the old man exclaimed.

I smiled for a moment. Then I frowned and said no more. Mira's father knew my father! I blushed. How complicated things could become!

"Good old Demosten! We were both wounded on the same day. They put us on a cart and drove us to the partisan field hospital. We were treated by a doctor—what was his name? Oh yes, Dr. Vasil Karakuli. I wonder what ever became of him?"

"I haven't heard of him in Tirana," I replied.

"How is Demosten anyway? I am getting a bit older," he said.

"He is fine. He has aged, too," I added.

"Good old Demosten! Tell him that Take Doko sends his regards. Tell him we were wounded together and treated by the same doctor, Vasil Karakuli," said the old man.

The fact that my father had been wounded with Take Doko upset me more than anything. Without knowing it, my father was wounding an old comrade, someone who had lain beside him in a field hospital and who had served in the same battalion. I shivered at the thought. The old man followed his daughter's footsteps. It was a cold February day.

"Mira," I said, "where are you going?"

"My father is going to visit an old friend of his and I am taking him there," she explained.

"I'm going to ask him if there is anything he can do at the conservatory to help," he said. "It's not the girl's fault. She is a good student. I don't believe a word they said. I may be old-fashioned, but I don't believe it at all. They say she has fallen in with a group of bad girls and all sorts of other things."

"Who said that?" I exclaimed, forgetting myself momentarily.

The old man, startled at the tone of my voice, stopped and looked at me apprehensively.

"Someone at the dean's office. Wait a moment, I've forgotten his name."

"Durgut!" said Mira in a weary voice.

"Yes, that's right, Durgut," repeated the old man.

"How dare he!" I cried passionately.

"You think so, too? It's nothing but gossip, I tell you. Your fellow students said so," he added, turning to his daughter. I noticed a new gleam in his eye. He shook his head slowly, smiled, and said, "Gossip!"

I began to admire this man who had such faith in his daughter. I had expected to find an old man furious at his daughter, a father come to tear her hair out in front of Durgut. Instead he shrugged off the accusations with one word: "gossip."

THE APPASSIONATA

135

We stood at the bus stop. Take Doko told Mira to go back to the residence, that he would visit his friend alone. Mira looked at me and turned to her father, saying, "Are you going to spend the night at a hotel or at your friend's place?"

"I imagine Nasi will insist that I stay," the father said and got onto the bus.

We waited until the bus departed and began to walk. The sky was cold and gray. There was snow in the air.

"My poor father," said Mira.

"What's happening, Mira?" I asked, feigning ignorance.

Mira trembled as if she were frozen.

"It is all so unbelievable. Durgut called me to his office this morning and accused me of indecent behavior. He said that you had gone down the drain because of me and that I was responsible for impeding the education of a cadre. He also claimed that I had brought other girls to the conservatory to meet the male students and that we had been spending our afternoons in 'immoral' activities. He said I would have to post a statement of self-criticism on the notice board, saying that I had recognized my errors, that I would put an end to my immoral ways, and that I would not see you again. Otherwise I would be expelled from the conservatory. He notified my father, too. Of course he didn't tell him everything he told me. He beat around the bush.

"I have never been so insulted!" said Mira, biting her lower lip and with tears welling in her eyes.

"Are you really going to put a statement on the notice board?" I asked.

Mira looked at me in amazement.

"The statement of self-criticism Durgut wants? How could you think I would do such a thing, Arthur?"

I took her arm and drew her toward me.

"You mustn't write so much as a word! It's all nonsense. I won't allow such slander to spread, no matter who started it. Don't worry, Mira!" I said, stroking her hair. She stood silent and I could feel a sense of relief in her.

"Arthur, I am embarrassed to suggest it, but could it be your father who made these accusations?"

My right shoulder twitched as if she had struck me.

"You mustn't think that, Mira! I'm going to get to the heart of the matter myself," I said without explaining any further.

We walked for a while in silence, each of us pondering. Until then, my only worry had been how to quit the conservatory, but now, new and much more complicated problems had arisen. Yes, my father was behind it all!

When it got dark, I accompanied Mira back to the residence and returned home.

8

I found my father lying in his pajamas on the kitchen sofa. He had his glasses on and was reading a book. He did not raise his head as I entered. My mother told me that Burhan had been looking for me again. I said nothing. I sat down at the table with my forehead in my hands.

I had a headache.

"Where have you been?" my mother inquired.

"I went for a walk in town," I replied coldly.

My father said nothing. Looking at him on the sofa reminded me of Mira's father, who had lain beside him in the field hospital. I tried to imagine my father as a partisan. Even now when the weather was damp he would complain of the aching caused by the scar.

"Take Doko sends his greetings," I said suddenly.

He didn't hear me. I repeated what I had said. My father raised his head. "Take Doko? Is that right?"

My father put his book down. He stretched his legs, stood up, and wrinkled his brow.

"Take Doko? I think I remember him," he said with his eyes fixed on the wall.

"I met him by chance and he told me to convey his greetings to you. You were together in a partisan field hospital," I said.

"Oh, yes! We were both wounded on the same day. We were together in one trench. A shell exploded right next to us and we were both wounded. That was a quarter of a century ago. Take Doko! He was a good fighter. Quite the hero! Why didn't you invite him home? We could have talked about old times," said my father, lost in memories.

I was fiddling with a pencil on the table, deep in thought.

"If only you had invited him over," said my father.

I raised my head slowly and looked my father in the eyes. He looked back at me. We seemed to be studying one another.

"I should have invited him over?" I asked without blinking. "I couldn't have. I would have been too ashamed," I said.

A nerve twitched on my father's face, near his nose.

"What do you mean, ashamed, Arthur?"

"I would have been ashamed, Father. You have wounded Take Doko to the quick!" I said.

"We were both wounded by the same mortar shell. You are talking nonsense!" said my father.

"Take Doko is Mira's father."

My father blushed. He ran his fingers through his hair and wiped off the droplets which were breaking out on his forehead. I studied him in silence. His face turned redder and was already covered in sweat. He sat up slowly on the sofa. The redness on his face vanished and he grew pale. My mother became anxious. She knew nothing about Mira's troubles. She bit her lip and looked at me reproachfully for having upset my father. She came over and laid her hand on his shoulder.

"You had better lie down, Demo!" she said and turned to me. "What is wrong with you, Arthur? Must you always upset your father? The two of you are constantly at one another's throats."

"We weren't fighting. I spoke quite calmly," I countered.

"Calm words can hurt all the more," she said.

My father rose again, speechless, opened the door, gave me a look full of pain and suffering, and turned away. My mother, unnerved, followed him into the bedroom.

The clock on the kitchen table was more audible than ever. I sat there counting each tick. From the bedroom I could hear my father's low voice, a succession of sighs and lamentations, interrupted only by my mother's own sighing. The clock talked to me in the only word it knew: "Ticktock!"

■ □ ■ □ ■

ABOUT THE AUTHORS

DRITËRO AGOLLI was head of the Albanian Union of Writers and Artists from the purge of Fadil Paçrami and Todi Lubonja at the Fourth Plenary Session in 1973 until 1992 and has had a significant influence on contemporary Albanian literature. Agolli was born in 1931 to a peasant family in Menkulas, in the Devoll region near Korça, and finished secondary school in Gjirokastra in 1952. He later continued his studies at the Faculty of Arts of the University of Leningrad and took up journalism upon his return to Albania, working for the daily newspaper *Zëri i Popullit* (*The People's Voice*) for fifteen years. Sixteen of his short stories were published in English in the volume *Short Stories* (Tirana 1985). One early collection of tales, *Zhurma e erërave të dikurshme* (*The Noise of Winds of the Past;* Tirana 1964), had the distinction of being banned and "turned into cardboard." The author was accused of Soviet revisionism at a time when the Party had called for more Maoist revolutionary concepts in literature and greater devotion to the working masses. Though Agolli was a leading personage in the Communist nomenclature, he remained a highly respected figure of public and literary life after the fall of the dictatorship and is still one of the most widely read authors in Albania. Among his recent volumes of prose are the short-story collection *Njerëz të krisur* (*Insane People;* Tirana 1995), the novel *Kalorësi lakuriq* (*The Naked Horseman;* Tirana 1996), and *Arka e djallit* (*The Devil's Box;* Tirana 1997).

MIMOZA AHMETI is from Kruja and was born in 1963. She is one of the enfants terribles of Albanian literature who, in the nineties, set about to expand her horizons and explore the possibilities offered to her by her own senses. Dragging the nation along the bumpy road to Europe, in her own idiosyncratic manner, she has managed in recent years to provoke Albania's impoverished and weary society into much-needed reflection which, with time, may lead to new and more sincerely human values. Although Ahmeti had written two volumes of verse in the late eighties, it was the fifty-three poems in the collection *Delirium* (Tirana 1994) which caught the public's attention. Among her prose works are the very short novel *Arktirau* (*The Architrave;* Tirana 1993) and *Absurdi koordinativ* (*The Coordinative Absurd;* Tirana 1996). Her works have recently been translated into Italian, Spanish, and French.

YLLJET ALIÇKA was born in Tirana in 1951. Since 1997 he has been working for the Delegation of the European Community in Albania. Aliçka is the author of two volumes of prose: *Tregime* (*Tales;* Tirana 1997) and *Kompromisi* (*The Compromise;* Tirana 2000). A collection of his short stories has also appeared in French as *Les slogans de pierres* (*The Slogans in Stone;* Castelnau-le-Lez 1999). The tale "The Slogans in Stone" has been filmed and was awarded the Youth Prize at the 2001 Cannes Film Festival.

LINDITA ARAPI was born in Lushnja in 1972. She began publishing poetry in literary magazines in 1989. Her first collection, *Kufomë lulesh* (*Corpse of Flowers;* Tirana 1993), received first prize in the Albanian poetry competition in Puglia, Italy. This was followed by the poetry volumes *Ndodhi në shpirt* (*It Happened in My Soul;* Elbasan 1995) and *Melodi të heshtjes* (*Melodies of Silence;* Peja 1998). A literature graduate of the University of Tirana, Arapi managed the poetry program sponsored by the Soros Foundation. She was a resident in the International Writers Program at the University of Iowa in 1996, finished her doctorate in Vienna in 2001, and currently lives in Cologne, Germany.

EQREM BASHA is among the most respected contemporary writers of Kosova in recent years. He was born in Dibra in 1948, in the Albanian-speaking western region of what is now the Republic of Macedonia, but his life and literary production are intimately linked to Kosova and its capital, Prishtina, where he has lived and worked for the past three decades. He is the author of eight volumes of innovative verse spanning the years 1971 to 1995, three volumes of short stories, and numerous translations (of French literature and drama in particular). He is currently in the publishing industry in Prishtina. A volume of his tales was recently published in French as *Les ombres de la nuit et autres récits du Kosovo* (*The Shades of the Night* *and Other Tales from Kosovo;* Paris 1999), and a collection of his poetry has appeared in English as *Neither a Wound nor a Song* (New York 2003). "The Snail's March Toward the Light of the Sun" was inspired by the actual experience of Kosova Albanian political prisoners in a Serb prison in the early 1990s.

STEFAN ÇAPALIKU was born in 1965 in Shkodra. He studied Albanian language and literature at the University of Tirana from 1984 to 1988 and received a doctorate in Albanian literature in 1995. He has taught at the University of Shkodra and worked for the Albanian Ministry of Culture. Çapaliku is the author of poetry and prose, as well as essays and literary studies. Among his major publications are the novel *Kronikë në lindje* (*Chronicle at Birth;* Shkodra 1996); the studies *Prijës për gjeografinë dhe sociologjinë e letërsisë shqiptare* (*Guide to Geography and Sociology in Albanian Literature;* Shkodra 1997) and *Letërsia e interpretuar: prijës për metodat bashkëkohore të leximit dhe studimit të letërsisë* (*Interpreted Literature: Guide to Contemporary Methods in Reading and Studying Literature;* Tirana 1998); the short story collection *Tregime për Anën* (*Tales for Anna;* Tirana 2002); drama in *Pesë drama dhe një korn anglez* (*Five Plays and an English Horn;* Tirana 2003); and the study *Estetika moderne* (*Modern Aesthetics;* Tirana 2004). Some of his literary works have been translated into French and Polish.

ELVIRA DONES was born in the ancient port city of Durrës in 1960. She studied at the University of Tirana and worked for a time in the television and film industries there. In 1988 she managed to flee the country, then still under Stalinist rule, and took up residence in Switzerland. She now works as a documentary filmmaker and screenwriter, based in Washington, D.C. Her first novel, *Dashuri e huaj* (*A Foreign Love;* Tirana 1997), was followed by *Kardigan* (*Cardigan;* Tirana 1998), the short story collection *Lule të gabuara* (*Mistaken Flowers;* Tirana 1999), and the explosive novel *Yjet nuk vishen kështu* (*Stars Don't Dress Up Like That;* Elbasan 2000), which has been translated into French and Italian. Much of her writing, not without autobiographical elements, deals with the theme of women as emigrants.

FATOS KONGOLI has recently become one of the most convincing representatives of contemporary Albanian literature. He was born in Elbasan in 1944 and studied mathematics in China during the tense years of the Sino-Albanian alliance. Kongoli chose not to publish any major works during the dictatorship. Instead, he devoted his creative energies to an obscure and apolitical career as a mathematician and waited for the storm to pass. His narrative talent and individual style only really emerged in the nineties, after the fall of the Communist dictatorship. His first major novel, *I humburi* (*The Loser;* Tirana 1992), is set in March 1991. This was followed by *Kufoma* (*The Corpse;* Tirana 1994), the story of another loser caught up in the inhumane machinery of the last decade of the Stalinist dictatorship in Albania; *Dragoi i fildishtë* (*The Ivory Dragon;* Tirana 1999), which focuses primarily on the life of an Albanian student in China in the 1960s; and *Lëkura e qenit* (*The Dog Skin;* Tirana 2003), a tale of love and forgotten affections. Kongoli's prose has been translated into French, German, Italian, Greek, and Slovak.

TEODOR LAÇO, from the village of Dardha (near Korça), where he was born in 1936, established his reputation as a significant prose writer of the socialist period with his novel *Tokë e ashpër* (*Rough Land;* Tirana 1971), which dealt with the collectivization of agriculture in mountain regions. The author was head of the New Albania Film Studio and, after the fall of the dictatorship, became chairman of the Social-Democratic parliamentary group. He has since published at least a dozen collections of short stories, five other novels, and numerous plays. Laço's short stories have appeared in *Portat e dashurisë* (*The Gates of Love;* Tirana 1980), *Një ditë dhe një jetë* (*A Day and a Life;* Tirana 1983), *Një dimër tjetër* (*Another Winter;* Tirana 1986), *Zemërimi i një njeriu të urtë* (*The Wrath of a Sage Man;* Tirana 1990), and *Mozaik dashurish* (*Mosaic of Loves;* Tirana 1998). Another collection was published in English under the title *A Lyrical Tale in Winter* (Tirana 1988).

FATOS T. LUBONJA is a writer, journalist, and often controversial intellectual figure who was born in Tirana in 1951. His father, Todi Lubonja, general director of Albanian radio and television, was purged in 1974. That same year, Fatos Lubonja, who had just graduated in theoretical physics from the University of Tirana, was arrested himself and sentenced to seven years' imprisonment for "agitation and propaganda" after police found writings criticizing the regime of Enver Hoxha in his uncle's attic. He began serving his sentence in the copper mine of Spaç. In 1979, while still incarcerated, he was sentenced to a further sixteen years in prison and was only released in 1991. Lubonja was a major force in the democracy movement in the early 1990s. In 1994, he founded the critical cultural periodical *Përpjekja* (*The Endeavor*), which caused a fury in many circles. His experience in the

Communist prison camps has been described in his memoirs: *Në vitin e shtatëmbëdhjetë* (*In the Seventeenth Year;* Tirana 1994) and *Ridënimi* (*The Second Sentence;* Tirana 1996). The latter has been translated into English, but remains unpublished. Fatos Lubonja is also the author of the drama *Ploja e mbramë* (*The Final Slaughter;* Tirana 1994), written in Burrel prison in 1988 and 1989, and of *Liri e kërcënuar: publicistika e viteve 1991–1997* (*Threatened Freedom: Current Affairs Writings from the Years 1991–1997;* Tirana 1999). In 2002, Lubonja was awarded the prestigious Italian Alberto Moravia Prize for international literature and in 2004 the equally prestigious Herder Prize for literature, in Hamburg.

KIM MEHMETI is a leading and innovative prose writer from the Albanian community in Macedonia. He was born in 1955 in Gërçec, near Skopje, where he now lives and works. He is the author of eleven volumes of prose, including *Lulehëna* (*Moon Flower;* Peja 1997), *Fshati i fëmijve të mallkuar* (*The Village of the Damned Children;* Peja 1998), and *Ritet e Nishanes* (*Nishane's Rites;* Peja 2004). One of his novels has appeared in German, *Das Dorf der verfluchten Kinder* (*The Village of the Damned Children;* Klagenfurt 2002). Mehmeti also writes in Macedonian and translates between Macedonian and Albanian.

■ □ ■ □ ■

WRITINGS FROM AN UNBOUND EUROPE

For a complete list of titles, see the Writings from an Unbound Europe Web site at www.nupress.northwestern.edu/ue.